Crimson Succubus
-The Demon Chronicles-

by Carmine

I0531496

Published by Logical Lust Publications © 2008 All rights reserved.

1st Edition. ISBN: 978-1-905091-14-0

$11.95 US
£6.95 UK

Cover image by E. H. Madden, www.pixelarcana.com.
© Logical Lust Publications 2008

📖

Tales of the Crimson Succubus
-The Demon Chronicles-

by Carmine

Contents

Mytoessa's Tales:

Publication History

Foreword

A few years back, I began receiving emailed submissions to the erotic literary ezine *Sauce*Box* from a writer known to me only as "Carmine." These submissions were short pieces ("flash-fiction," if you will) detailing yet another "Tale of the Crimson Succubus." Each was a stand-alone jewel, horrible, cruel, fantastically, outrageously, graphically sexual, but also somehow (dare I say it . . . forgive me, Carmine) charming. I liked them very much and published every one that was sent.

Now I find that some of these short tales along with longer pieces concerning the "adventures" of the Crimson Succubus, and a third section concerning a mythical nymph Mytoessa who also becomes involved with the succubus have been collected together in one place—a delightfully, tastefully disgusting book, **Tales of the Crimson Succubus, The Demon Chronicles** by Carmine.

This person, Carmine, is one sick puppy, but one with adorable eyes and floppy ears. The tales involve much blood- and semen-letting, murder, torture, deception and pain, but at the same time, I often want to laugh and wish that the creatures would appear for real, in front of me, so that I could see with my own eyes and even touch (very, very carefully, mind you) these monsters formed from the primordial slime of all of our great cultural myths.

And of course, like all myths, these tales speak to our deepest fears, and hopes and fantasies . . . perhaps to archetypes from times before even the written word, times long forgotten in consciousness but remembered in the collective genetic code. I don't know. Whatever. They're a great read, an exciting read and one that will tickle your nightmares and daydreams long after you've put this book down.

Guillermo Bosch.

Author of **Rain** and **The Passion of Muhammad Shakir**

A Word of Explanation

I anticipate that you have acquired this book because you have read one or two tales of the beguiling she-devil known as Crimson Succubus. For those bold and curious souls whose insatiable curiosity led to the purchase of this book, I believe I owe you a short description of Crimson Succubus:

One of the lesser-known angels to fall with Lucifer at the climax of the battle between heaven and hell, Crimson Succubus imbues wanton desire without measure. Known as a Lilim—one of Lilith's daughters -- Succubus was taught the ways of lasciviousness and carnality. It was she who first beguiled monks within darkened abbeys, so that these poor self-professed celibates wrapped rosaries around their members in a feeble attempt to ward off her nocturnal defilement.

Other rumors about this she-devil abound: Succubus is said to have whispered into the ear of the Marquis de Sade, inspired Aleister Crowley's infamous Scarlet Woman, and spawned the Night Hags, her servants that to this day inspire lust within all humanity. It is also believed that this creature now torments the once-pious Carmine with nightly dreams of decadence, which he must make known to all kindred souls.

This book consists of three sections. The first of these sections is made up of vignettes that are exactly one hundred words, no more, no less (this count does not include the title). These short pieces are called flash fiction, microfiction, or teaser tales. The stories detailing the carnal exuberance of Crimson Succubus began as flash fiction, with many of the tales appearing in online magazines known as *Amoret, XtreXmeX, and BDSM Cafe*. Savor these like a glass of fine wine. If liquor is not to your liking, then think of these as Zen-like parables in which the outcome tickles something else entirely...

The second section of this collection collects for the first time the longer stories written under the Succubus banner. These stories exist simply because they had to be told.

The third section is dedicated to a character I created when writing this series. Named after a nymph, Mytoessa spent her youth under the watchful eye of the dryad Nimue who taught her the simple ways of nature. Unfortunately, a war between King Harald's kingdom of Fria and several neighboring realms led to the destruction of the forest. The conflict destroyed many faeries, including Nimue, who refused to abandon her tree as the forest was engulfed in flames.

While seeking out those who destroyed her family and home, Mytoessa discovered the underlying source of the chaos: Crimson Succubus. Armed with a demon-smiting blade, Mytoessa relentlessly pursues the she-devil and anyone who would dare associate with such an amoral creature.

This book collects for the first time the only full-length tales written about Mytoessa and her fairy kingdom.

It is my sincere hope that you enjoy this collection. Yours in eternity, I remain. . . .

--Carmine

To the Devil, a Daughter

Come here, my darling,
and sit by our fire
Set free inhibition,
let loose your desire
Feel how the flames burst
within this tenebrous pyre
Savor each struggling ember,
climbing higher and higher

Our mouth it consumes you,
your lips fall apart
We lick all of your being
so sweet yet so tart
We battle with chastity
we rip it apart
Give us your maidenhead
open your heart!

Descendant of Lillith
we dip in your well
Our precious little Lilim
our harlot from hell
Thrust after thrust
clanging your bell
Spill our licentious seed
cerise burns o'er your shell

Cremate the body,
ashes to dust
We unleash this delight,
for unleash we must
A creature of unbridled cunning
and lascivious lust
A sanguine she-devil
our Crimson Succubus

- Flash Fiction -

After Sodom and Gomorrah

Two women emerged from a cave. The older of the two knelt before a puddle and splashed her face. The younger one closed her eyes.

When she opened them, there stood before her an androgynous angel with umber skin. It reached for her, delicate arms cradling her in a soft embrace.

The older woman gasped. "Dearest sister," she screamed, "one of the angels has returned!"

The angel stuck out a forked tongue and licked the younger girl's lips.

"Salty," she teased, clasping its crotch. "Just like your mother."

Succubus then eyed the older woman. "What say you, begetter of Moabites?"

In Mockery of the Angel of Death

The she-demon Naamah knelt before the Dark One. In her blistered hands she held some dust.

"What is this?"

"I treaded upon the Earth, and it beseeched me, 'Do not take anything from me to make someone who will be punished forever.'"

Before the Dark One could show his displeasure, Crimson Succubus crawled into the megaron. The she-devil's body glistened with gobs of an alabaster fluid.

"And this?" the Dark One roared.

"I treaded upon the Earth, and from the men I commanded: Deliver up your souls."

The Dark One grinned. "With this shall I mold my minions of clay."

The Estuary

Lord Draco gasped as Crimson Succubus mounted his member. Draco made several furtive thrusts, but the she-devil would have none of it. She pinned his arms to the stone altar and clamped her thighs against his hips.

"Bite me." Succubus leaned forward and offered a breast.

Draco teased her nipple with sharp teeth.

"Weakling!" she roared. "Draw blood!"

Furious, Draco tore into her breast, his clenched teeth bringing away flesh. Moments later, he relinquished his seed.

"Now," whispered Succubus. "We shall become the estuary between heaven and hell."

When the cock's brackish fluid touched her wound, angel and devil burned.

Bringer of Light

Crimson Succubus knelt before Lucifer, her eyes downcast. In turn, Lucifer looked down at her, his gnarled hands clasped around an enormous member.

"I have heard that you question one of my titles, "he muttered between bowel-grinding grunts.

"My Lord," Succubus began.

"Silence!" he bellowed. "Stare into my snake's divine mouth."

As Lucifer pleasured himself, the she-devil stared into the abyss. The cock's gaping hole beckoned her closer, and so enthralled was she that everything became shadow.

A sudden burst of liquid light almost blinded her.

"I am the Light Bringer," Lucifer affirmed.

Bathed in his luminosity, Succubus cooed.

Fall of the Grigori

Arazyael stood upon a boulder and stretched his wondrous wings. He so yearned for the halls of heaven.

At the rock's base stood Crimson Succubus, who masqueraded as one of the daughters of Eve. She reached out and clasped the angel's mammoth member, but he paid her no heed.

"I am the noon of God," he whispered.

"Were you not sent here to live among us?" her forked tongue weaved.

"And we have shown your kind much."

"Then let me show you something." The she-devil knelt before Arazyael's cock and brought it to life.

And so lust became Arazyael's midnight.

Thelema's Babalon Working: The Contents of a Man's Chalice

Father Matthias wakened before dawn and stared at the moldering wall across from his bed. Upon the rancid plaster writhed an amalgamation of deformed creatures engaged in infinite forms of debauchery.

Matthias closed his eyes and began to recite Psalm 23: "Thou anointest my head with oil," he spat out. "My cup runneth over."

"Thy tears, thy sweat, thy blood, thy semen, thy love, thy faith shall provide," countered a voice in the dark. "Ah, I shall drain thee like the cup that is of me."

Matthias screamed as Babylon's crimson-skinned whore tightened the rosary beads about his polluted instrument.

War of Words

Lord Draco groaned as Crimson Succubus milked the dregs of his pungent juice from a still-firm member. The she-devil turned her head and spat the spunk onto the stone floor of the castle.

"Why the vulgar display, dearest?" the warrior inquired.

"You remind me of old poetic verses that I'd just soon forget," Succubus said, her eyes ablaze.

"Oh? Why?"

"They feel so good at first, but in the end, the aftertaste diminishes their value."

Draco smiled. "And so it is that you remind me of campaigns yet waged."

"How so?" Succubus teased.

"With each climax I weaken my enemy."

The Imp of the Perverse

A middle-aged man stared at the demon before him. Leaden eyes watched as she licked the remnants of his seed from her lips. Despite his best efforts, he grew aroused again.

The she-devil opened her mouth and eased a finger down her throat. Upon its withdrawal she began to crawl toward the man.

"Shall we have at it again, dear pilgrim?" she cooed.

"Aye," he sighed. "But upon wakening, I shall confess this sin to my beloved wife."

"So the chains will fall," Succubus said as she spat on his bulbous helmet. "And tomorrow you shall be fetterless—but where?"

A Monk's Holy Water

For several days Brother Matthias knelt before a statue of Christ. He gazed at the monastery's ceiling while down below a succubus worked her wickedness.

"May the Holy Cross be my light, Saint Benedict," he said between clenched teeth. "Let not the dragon lead me. Step back, minion of Satan!"

"What you offer me is evil," Crimson Succubus mocked him, her nails digging into his aroused member. "Drink the poison yourself."

"No!" The monk ejaculated, his seed filling the demon's maw.

"Salt and water." The she-devil swallowed deep.

"*Nunquam suade mihi vana*," the monk said as the sanguine devil vanished.

The Serpent That Cannot be Charmed

Lord Draco stood at the top of a tower. Naked to the world, he stroked his cock with gnarled hands. A storm beckoned in the distance as wind caressed the warrior's battle-scarred frame.

Carried in the gales was a most delicate voice. "Have you made your nest in the roots of the tree?" it whispered to him.

"I have not the wisdom of Gilgamesh!" he screamed as the storm grew stronger.

Raindrops pelted his flesh, their resonance driving him mad. Still, he refused to ejaculate.

And so Crimson Succubus, like her wicked mother Lilith, took refuge within the man's trunk.

Feeding the She-Devil

Father Warden watched as men entered a shack reputed to belong to the village harlot. When a man emerged from the abode, his trousers were stained. Having seen enough, the cleric stormed into the shack.

"Sinners!" he screamed.

But there was no woman inside. Instead, he saw a man insert his member into an incantation bowl. Moments later, he withdrew, the remnants of his seed evident on a withering cock.

"What sorcery is this?" Warden gasped.

"Wickedness possesses many forms," whispered an old man suddenly at the priest's side. "And so we feed her and placate the virile amongst us."

Of the Wanderer Matronit and Masturbation

A golden-haired beauty strolled through a forest. Leaning against a tree, Crimson Succubus dropped an apple and motioned toward the curvaceous woman.

"Come hither," the she-devil beckoned. "I wish to know you."

"I am called Matronit, consort to the One Lord." The pristine beauty stared at the she-devil. "And are you Baphomet, for you possess breasts above and a serpent below?"

Succubus grinned as she stroked the snake. "Shall we become one, like my mother and your King?"

"Forever shall you be alone." Matronit sighed and walked away. "But not I."

In defiance, Succubus spat the seed of countless masturbators.

Seal of Solomon

Demon-huntress Mytoessa stepped into the dark chamber, her shimmering blade at the ready. Along the obsidian-like floor writhed a young woman whose hands tugged at strawberry nipples while dawn's dew tainted her crescent-shaped cleft.

Mytoessa's mouth and slit watered. She dropped the blade and stepped into the woman's sphere. She was accepted and both drank deep from each other's honey-filled well.

"You are mine," Crimson Succubus said as her flesh turned sanguine. "I did not think you could be so easily fooled."

"Seen from above, we form a hexagram." Mytoessa grinned as she licked. "It is you who are trapped."

Protection from the Night-Strangler

Demon-huntress Mytoessa stepped into the cursed home. Into the main room she wandered, her nipples growing hard. She willed herself into the child's room, where she dropped to one knee and forced an intense orgasm to pass through her.

"Any house that I enter, you shall not. And in any courtyard that I walk, you shall not."

Mytoessa crawled to the crib, where she placed a leather thong about the child's member. She pulled it taut as another orgasm struck her.

"My life for yours, little one."

Honeysweet fluid flowed down her thigh as the child cried for its mother.

Blaspheming the Tetragrammaton

Having assumed the pious form of a nun, Crimson Succubus knelt before a cleric in his personal bedchamber. While the priest clung to a rosary, the she-devil wrapped her arms around his pelvis.

"*Adonai!*" the priest screamed. "We do this only to celebrate life."

Succubus crawled under the priest's robe, where she gorged herself upon the man's once-celibate member.

She withdrew the sticky member from her gullet and growled, "Scream it!"

"Yahweh!" he screamed as down below his member relinquished its seed.

On all fours, Succubus wrote out "YHWH" with the priest's cum.

"Life is forsaken," she whispered triumphantly.

Amorous's Humor

Neophyte Lydia stood before Crimson Succubus's senior thrall, Amorous.

"May I speak, Mistress?" Lydia asked.

Amorous nodded, her eyes wide.

"I have heard that our Dark Queen entertains the forbidden. Thus, I wish to invoke necromancy, for it is said there are secrets amongst the dead."

Amorous took from an altar a thick jawbone. Without a word, she guided Lydia onto her lap where she pulled down her panties and eased the bone into the young woman's taut button.

"Do you see?" asked Amorous.

"I see nothing. Please, Mistress, enlighten me."

"I see a jawbone of an ass inside another!"

- Fiction -

Loving the Worm

Assuming the simple guise of a Spanish senorita, the she-devil Crimson Succubus entered a tavern by the name of "El Conquistador" and found a table in the darkest part of the establishment. Moments later, a dapper-looking waiter walked over, a bottle of clear liquor tucked under one arm.

"*Buenas tardes*. I am Fernando, your attendant for the evening. What may I get you, senorita?"

"Tequila, *por favor.*"

Before the waiter could turn around and attend to the order, Succubus locked her sanguine orbs on his diminutive eyes. Raw, carnal heat emanated from her countenance, permeating every pore of the young man. Using the sleeve of his tunic to wipe off the sweat building upon his brow and saturating his mane of obsidian-tainted hair, Fernando found that his entire pelvis pulsed like a troubled heart. The urge to look down was great, but he managed to ward off the temptation. Still, he felt his ass become increasingly tighter as his cock grew so large every inch ached and burned. These effects were so great his pants migrated upward, revealing his dilemma to all who would bother to look in his direction.

"A goblet," he managed to blurt out. "Forgive me. I shall fetch you one."

"No need," replied Succubus, her stare maintaining its somniferous intensity. "Relax, darling. Now, put the bottle down and remove the cork."

Red-faced and trembling, Fernando did as he was told. After taking in and releasing a most luscious sigh, Succubus began licking the bottle's head, her viperous tongue running along its lustrous edge.

20

"An excellent liquor." He tried to look away again, but her spell was much too strong.

"Where is the worm?" the she-devil wanted to know.

"Senorita, it is mezcal that contains a worm. And it is not really a worm at all, but rather a butterfly waiting to be released from its cocoon."

"It is said that the essence of this worm—or shall I say, this cocoon—invigorates the taste to aphrodisiacal heights."

His cock aching for release, the young man tugged on his trousers. "Yes, I have heard it said."

"Shall we make some mezcal, then?" Succubus pouted. "Or would you rather go home and try on your sister's dress, little boy?"

"Senorita?"

"You heard me."

Fernando's jaw clamped shut, his pelvis square with the rest of his sculpted frame.

Dropping to her knees, Succubus pulled down Fernando's pants only enough to expose his dark member. Immediately after taking a lick of salt and a bite of lime, the demon placed her lips on the waiter's engorged cock, teasing its mushroom-shaped head. She pushed forward, her lips parting. The salt along the edges of her mouth stung the cock, which in turn made it stretch even more.

"Delicious," she suspired, hissing the final consonant of the word. "An excellent vintage, Fernando."

As the young man arched his back, Succubus wrapped long fingernails around his taut bottom, their barbed tips digging into

21

each cheek. Opening her mouth just enough, she eased his cock within, her tongue swirling about its head while her cheeks squeezed the shaft.

The waiter tensed, climax swelling within his gut, and Succubus placed the cock's head into the bottle. She then methodically stroked and squeezed the shaft until his juice mixed with the alcohol.

"*Caramba*, the essence of a butterfly," she said, taking a swig. "It is mezcal now."

"What do you mean?" The waiter stared at his spent cock, his lips trembling.

"You were untouched by woman, until now."

The waiter's eyes watered. "I was to have been a priest."

For an instant, Fernando swore he saw the senorita's eyes turn completely red and short horns sprout above her brow. A blink later, however, the vision was gone.

"Come, I shall make you a priest."

Fernando froze.

"The first step is to make *sal de gusano*—worm salt, like what is made in Oaxaca." Succubus managed an impious grin. "It will cleanse you."

"Worm salt?"

"Mmmmm, yes. It consists of salt, chili powder, and worm. I love it with lime and orange slices."

Fernando's cock once again began to stir. "It will cleanse me?"

Succubus licked her lips. "Oh yes." She touched his forehead. "But not right now."

~ ~ ~ ~ ~ ~ ~ ~ ~

Church bells rang in a monastery and at once seminarians began their morning rituals. At the southwest corner of the abbey's dormitory, seminarian Fernando Salas opened his eyes and removed the singular blanket that covered his body. Sitting up, he unraveled the rosary attached to his cock's shaft. The crucifix was covered with his own alabaster seed.

When the bells stopped ringing, a hideous yet enchanting chuckle made its way through the dormitory, and in several instances senior disciples found themselves defiled with enormous erections of their own.

Wiping away the sin from his crotch, Fernando dressed and was about to make his way to the bathing area when he spotted several items on a desk. Placed on a plate adjacent to his working Bible were a phial of salt, a cruet filled with mashed chili powder, and several orange and lime slices. And there was a short note, the chirography as scarlet as blood.

"For tonight," Fernando read aloud.

Dropping to his knees, he screamed the abomination's name again and again.

"Lilim—daughter of Lilith!"

But it was fruitless. Fernando had learned about the love of the worm, and for as long as he lived there would be infinite recipes upon which to indulge.

Sanguine Maiden

For more than 30 years Elizabeth had been a self-imposed captive of Csejthe Castle. When she first set eyes upon the citadel, with its array of gates, towers, and siege machinery, she had been but 15 years of ascension. Her eccentric but deep-seated family, in an attempt to curb its incestuous proclivity, had married her off to a boorish yet affluent man-at-arms, and as a result the newly crowned countess spent great spans of time alone or in the company of disputable individuals.

A descendent of the powerful Hun Gutkeled clan, which controlled broad areas of East Central Europe, Elizabeth had led a sheltered yet opulent life, one filled with servile peasants, wallowing servants, and a complaisant retinue. Of her vassals, the most gentle and reverent was the one called Ruby Daimon, and it was she whom Elizabeth despised most.

On many occasions Elizabeth called upon the maid and had her stand next to a massive silver-plated mirror. From dawn to twilight the tall and lanky woman would stare at the servant and then at the mirror, her eyes becoming slits as the day wore on. What the countess searched for was unclear to the servant, for Elizabeth demanded absolute silence.

In 1604, a courier pierced the great doors of Csejthe. The young man bore solemn news: Elizabeth's husband had perished from stab wounds inflicted upon his countenance by a peculiarly vehement harlot from Bucharest. It seemed the warrior had refused to pay for services rendered, and as he turned to take his leave, the whore set upon him, blade in hand. For the remainder of the day and long into the night, the servants of the great keep heard Elizabeth in her room; the mistress was not mourning, but rather spent the majority of the hours cackling and babbling hysterically.

The following morning, Elizabeth sent for Ruby, and once again she instructed the young woman to stand by the mirror. The countess's almond-shaped eyes widened, for the insidious looking glass reflected not a young, angelic complexion, but rather a wan, heavily wrinkled semblance. She used the tips of her manicured nails to touch the limitless caverns upon her face, the middle digits tracing the furrows about her forehead, the wrinkles around her eyes, the rifts along her once-high cheekbones, and the folds surrounding her pallid lips. Removing a crimson turban, she discovered a mane of alabaster hair, its tresses spun like straw to the spool.

Tears traveling down her face, Elizabeth then turned her attention to Ruby, who as always stood motionless, her dominant hand resting upon the mirror's fulcrum. Her back straight and bosom pushed outward because of an overly tight leather corset, the servant smiled, her lips parting ever so slightly. Elizabeth closed her eyes, stood up, and then lashed out, her fingernails ripping into the poor girl's cheek.

"You dare beam at me, harridan!" Elizabeth brought her hand back, ready to strike again. "We are in mourning. See you not our lamentation garb?"

Almost instantly Ruby dropped to the floor. Prostrate, the girl reached out and touched Elizabeth's calf-molded boot. Taking notice that her gesture had been accepted, she moved inward slightly, wrapping her arm around the high shoe and placing her burning cheek upon its well-oiled leather.

"Forgive," whispered the handmaiden.

Elizabeth looked down and admired the little thrall. "Stand, our chastised vassal. Look upon us."

Ruby took to her feet, this time her eyes downcast and her frame bent forward slightly. Elizabeth smiled.

"Very good. You have pleased us."

25

Without thinking, Ruby touched her cheek and then brought the hand to her face, palm inward. The tip of the middle finger was coated with blood. She placed the finger close to her lips then used her tongue to wipe it clean. As she swallowed, the gash upon her cheek began to shimmer, at length sealing itself shut. Although the wound remained red, there was no scar, only fresh skin.

Elizabeth's eyes narrowed. "Is this your secret, then?"

Looking at her striking palm, Elizabeth discovered that some of the servant's blood had tainted her pale skin. Grinning, she licked away the vital fluid, hissing in response to its metallic taste. She then looked in the mirror; some of the wrinkles on her face were gone. Instead of her usual pasty aspect, her face had become soft once again, the milky flesh revitalized and fresh.

"Give it to us," she said turning to the handmaiden once again. "Make us young."

Crossing her arms, Ruby stared into Elizabeth's eyes. "You must give yourself to me."

"You are a fool!"

Elizabeth made to strike again, but this time Ruby caught the noblewoman's wrist. Before she could act, Ruby squeezed the flesh and bone, her Herculean grip taking Elizabeth down to her knees. She then stepped forward, thrusting her hips into Elizabeth's face.

"The key to eternity."

With her free hand Ruby lifted her peasant dress, revealing a pair of taut, honey-lined thighs, between which hung an engorged pair of fleshy lips. Ruby pulled Elizabeth upward, drawing her into the cleft.

"Taste me."

Elizabeth's lips parted and from within emerged a long, slender tongue. Seeing the pulpy appendage, Ruby tightened her grip and drew the woman forward, concurrently parting her luscious thighs. She then grasped Elizabeth's hair with both hands and mashed her face into her cleft. At first Elizabeth resisted, but the fragrance emanating from the servant touched her very soul. She had never breathed in its likeness, but its intoxicating essence hinted at imperishability.

Long-suppressed feelings coated Elizabeth with a thin layer of perspiration. Giving in to wantonness, she opened her mouth wide and used her flaccid lips to cup Ruby's cleft. She thrust her tongue into the flesh, piercing the lips and tasting the honey within. Wrapping her hands around the thrall's bottom, she drove ever inward, her tongue probing deeper and deeper. Eyes closed, Ruby moved the woman's head up and down. Elizabeth conceded, her tongue moving up and down the chasm, at times superficially and at others deeply. As Ruby's rhythm increased, Elizabeth flicked her tongue inside and out, at times forcing the lingua to undulate like a fish out of water.

Enveloped in the transudation of passion, Ruby stepped forward, wrapping her thighs around Elizabeth's head. For a moment Elizabeth panicked, but as Ruby squatted on her face, she felt oddly exhilarated. Flat on her back, the old woman extended her tongue as far as it could go. In response, Ruby ground her love-hole along Elizabeth's mouth, the friction erasing the slings and arrows of time.

"Yes, worship me," Ruby hissed through clenched teeth.

Slapping her cleft with satisfaction, Ruby stood up, bent down, and then helped Elizabeth rise to her feet. Overcome with emotion, Elizabeth embraced the servant, her face buried in the other's neck. Then her eyes met the mirror.

There, reflected off the looking glass, was no thrall, but rather an abomination spawned from hell. Disrobed and made of flesh, the thing was female, and yet it was something more. Thick tresses of ebon-tainted hair led to a pair of long shoulders, which in turn sprouted lithe arms. But where shoulder blades should be, there swelled a couple of leathery, bat-like wings. Below a curved lower back and above well-defined buttocks there grew a long, whip-like tail that ended in a trident-shaped nip. And then there was the creature's flesh: from head to toe the skin was as crimson as the blood that coursed through every man's heart.

Ruby—now revealed as the Lilim known as the Crimson Succubus—sunk her pointed spurs deep into Elizabeth's cheeks.

"Wish you to keep this new semblance, Countess?"

"Yes, we do."

"The secret shall you have, so long as you do my bidding."

"Our tongue shall we hold so long as homeliness sleeps in Sodom."

Crimson Succubus giggled. "So shall it be."

~ ~ ~ ~ ~ ~ ~ ~

For five years Elizabeth and her Night Hags roamed the countryside, hunting for virginal girls, who were then taken captive, hung—alive and naked, sometimes in devices known as iron maidens—and slowly drained of their precious blood. At first Elizabeth bathed in the vital fluid. In time she imbibed blood as it drained from a particularly juicy morsel, preferably a child whose face foretold great beauty.

In the end, the countess caught the attention of Hungarian Emperor Matthias II, who ordered all the witches be burned alive, save Elizabeth. Because of her noble birth, he granted her a living death: she was forever sealed into a tiny closet within her lush castle. For several years Countess Elizabeth Bathory lived under such brutal confinement.

Upon her death, she left instructions that the following be carved into her gravestone:

Beauty is to reflection

As blood is to dust;

The minion is Beth Bathory;

The mistress, Crimson Succubus.

The Demon Chronicles: Kuru-pira

For as long as the stronghold of Trin had stood stalwart, the knight known as Rosate had been its principal defender. A cunning warrior and nonpareil man-at-arms, Rosate for most of his life had indulged upon a variety of forbidden desires driven by a most insatiable carnality. It was also well known that this great knight scorned maidens, his tastes leaning more toward squires whose leggings accented virile pouches and well-sculpted rumps.

And so it was that Rosate's exploits soon could not easily be counted. Many a bard composed whimsy and soon the waggish verses reached the ears of King Bestal, whose very son Adam also had an affinity for what dangled between a youth's limber thighs. Through several trusted spies and one lovelorn courtier, Bestal learned of a rendezvous between his son and the great knight.

"Your Majesty," whispered one such spy into the king's wrinkled ear. "Your son Adam has been disgraced like far too many others, for Rosate refuses to relinquish his seed, instead vacating his lemon-tainted water upon the face of his squire of the moment. What of the kingdom, Majesty? Does it end with you?"

Bestal's wrath was immediate. With bare hands that had become iron from countless battles, he strangled the effeminate mole, who as he expired released a load of not golden but flaxen nectar.

At first the king wished to murder the knight as he had the milksop, but soon his brow was wrinkled and his frame grew still. At dawn he brought forth Solomon's ring of summoning. Standing within a circle of protection, he drew a blade across his palm and let blood drip onto the alabaster marble. As his most trusted sentinels sealed the megaron, the king began an arcane ritual designed to extract an insidious evil from the bowels of the Devil himself.

30

It was twilight before the creature known as the Crimson Succubus stepped into the starlit apex of the great megaron. Statuesque and beguiling, the she-devil spread her great wings and flicked her spiny tail. Black eyes stared at the king as ebon hair shunned the light.

"You called upon me, Majesty?" Wolf-like fangs shimmered.

"So, the Goetic powers abide still." The king nodded. "Good—I have something to discuss with you. My son, he fornicates amongst his own. And it has now been revealed to me that my greatest knight denigrates him by excreting upon his sovereign countenance."

Crimson Succubus chuckled. "And what would you have me do?"

"I beseech you, scarlet demon: Allow me to taste the nectar of retribution."

"There is a price, Sire."

"That is of no concern. Name it and it shall be yours."

Succubus nodded. "So shall it be done, Sire."

~ ~ ~ ~ ~ ~ ~ ~

The knight Rosate languished among several scores of multicolored cushions while several disrobed squires rolfed his muscular frame. Lost to the muse, he twirled one end of a long black mustache with his dominant hand while with the other he impaled a squire's lush mouth onto his thick arrow of love. The young man's tongue swirled round and round Rosate's mushroom arrowhead, and when the knight stiffened, the squire swallowed him whole, only to fall back, gagging, as golden fluid leaked from his mouth and onto the granite parterre.

"You are bathed in my waste," Rosate chuckled as he reached for a goblet filled with mead. "Fool, you should take your fill, for my strength flows even in this golden fluid."

Downing the mead and demanding another, Rosate used his sword hand to stroke his love-arrow, working the shaft with dexterous fingers. As the bolt blossomed again, the knight took notice of a new squire, an exquisite Adonis who stood at the other end of the great hall.

"Come hither," he bellowed.

Smiling with coquettish abandon, the libidinous creature made his way through the vomitorium and into the great hall. Dressed in a silver toga, the young man shimmered like well-wrought armor. Flaming red hair sat atop a face chiseled by ancient masters, for his features were pliant even under the garish light of the hall. He was lithe yet well formed, his muscles interlocked and flexing as he moved.

"And you are?" Rosate belched. "Your name, boy!"

"I am called Kuru, my master."

"Remove that frock, Kuru."

"As you wish, Lord."

As the garment fell onto the floor, Rosate could not help himself. Wiping away saliva from his lips, he stared anew at the ambrosial site before him. Kuru's love-arrow was a thing of beauty. Long, slender, and almost alabaster in tone, its shaft was bereft of down, its texture like an infant's tender flesh. At the end of the engorged dart was a chanterelle-shaped arrowhead, its tip glistening with ardor's dew.

Dropping to his knees, Rosate cupped his hands around Kuru's firm rump, easing the squire toward him as he closed his eyes and parted his lips in anticipation. Arching his back, Kuru placed his hands on the knight's shoulders as his swollen shaft pierced its target. Squeezing his scrumptious butt cheeks together, he rammed into Rosate's orifice. The knight opened wider, letting the squire drive his inflamed arrow down his scorched throat.

"Lord," the squire moaned.

Kuru's fingernails dug into Rosate's shoulders. The knight wrapped his lips around the flesh, refusing to let go. The squire screamed, driving the shaft into its target one final time. Eyes still closed, Rosate felt Kuru's volcanic eruption. The knight swallowed as much as he could, but soon the juice was running down the sides of his mouth.

The juice was golden.

At once Rosate retched, his tongue extended outward as fluid dripped onto the floor. Wiping his face clean, he stood up and screamed for his sword.

"To quench, or not to quench," hissed a voice.

Across from him was not the Adonis Kuru, but rather a hideous abomination. The thing stood upright like a man, yet it was not a man. Long locks of filth-laden hair hung down from a massive head, its countenance consisting of two goat horns, a pair of slit eyes, a bulbous nose, and a wide mouth from which could be seen dagger-like fangs. A hirsute torso sprouted two slender arms, at the ends of which were not fingers but scimitar-like spurs. Below an emaciated gut were two sinewy legs that belonged more to a ram. The only thing that remained of the Adonis Kuru was the love-arrow, which even now remained suffused with lasciviousness.

"I am called Kuru-pira," the demon stated. "I have come for you."

Rosate's blade became molten before his eyes. He fell to his knees again, only this time he clutched at his throat. The golden fluid from the demon—it was mephitic as a viper's kiss.

"I am nine in the twelfth legion," Kuru-pira continued. "King Bestal sends his greetings."

"Adam?"

"Fret not, for my mistress has plans for him."

"Mistress?"

The demon nodded in affirmation. "Crimson Succubus."

Without any further concern, the knight fell to one side and became still.

~ ~ ~ ~ ~ ~ ~ ~

A cerise-skinned woman walked into Prince Adam's bedchamber. Eyes downcast, she waited until he acknowledged her presence. Vitreous eyes looked her way, their insides burning with bluish flames. The maid smiled, nonchalantly wiping away a trickle of blood that stained her chin.

"Your bath, dear prince. I have drawn it for you."

"You again?" For a moment, the young man's eyes widened, but soon they were glassy once again. "Yes, my bath. It is time."

As the prince entered the bathing chamber, he could smell the effervescence of the liquid, which bubbled like the aqua vitae of the gods. At once he descended into the whirling pool and began covering himself with the intoxicating liquid.

Crimson Succubus stifled a laugh as she watched from outside the chamber. Covered with the sanguine fluid of several scores of crucified bleeders, the prince relished the smell, texture, and sight

34

of it all. Opening his mouth, Adam unveiled a pair of pointed fangs. With relish he began drinking the blood around him.

"The dead do not suffer, nor do they easily forgive their fathers," the she-devil muttered as she went about her business.

Master of Ropes

Long lost to the modern world, the temple had once been home to an order of monks who had transcended Zen. These cenobites had moved on, and so it came to pass that other arts were taught within the shrine's power-laden walls. Some of the arts were forbidden, but the isolation of the place ensured that few interlopers ever learned of the secrets taught there.

The she-devil called the Crimson Succubus was not an interloper, but she was in fact an avatar of taboo. And so she had been drawn to this place of secrets, her heart aching for prohibited knowledge and boundless torment. The seductive creature knelt before Waotaka Makino, a Japanese master of ropes.

"You have come a long way." Makino observed as he smoked a long ivory pipe carved with intricate designs. "What do you seek, little demon?"

"Excruciating pain, Master."

"Is that so?" Makino chuckled. "Come inside."

After stripping the creature so that she stood naked, Makino then prepared several ropes by soaking them in an unknown emulsion. He then asked the she-demon to stand in the great hall. There she stood until the megaron had grown dark, at which time Makino returned. He said nothing but immediately set to work.

The ancient one began by wrapping a rope directly under Succubus's bust, the first two windings between breasts and body. Another rope was wrapped around the top of her breasts so that it pressed them against the lower windings. Yet another rope worked its way between the swelled udders, each line's end over one shoulder and tied under the bottom windings on her back.

With each breath she took, the ropes lifted, teased, and massaged her bosom.

"This is called *shinju*, for it is breast *shibari*."

"And I care, why?"

Ignoring his charge, Makino then concentrated on her lower body, tying a cord just below her waist. He then slipped a second cord halfway through the first cord, wove it carefully between her legs, and tied three special knots, each large enough to titillate her navel, love slit, and round bottom.

And finally, a suspension rope was tied to the main ropes. With the patience of a mortifier of the flesh, Makino pulled on the rope, watching as the knots grew tighter and the ropes dug into flesh. It was a long time before Succubus hung from the temple's rafters.

"This is nothing!" The she-devil crooned with delight. "Bastard, I wanted pain!"

Makino grinned. "You are a most elaborate *ikebana*—a flower arrangement. You shall give pleasure to all my guests, for every night I shall hold a sumptuous repast in this very room. Their eyes shall gaze upon you, a thing of beauty. Ah, a true *ikebana*. Is this not a demon's pain?"

Makino's words were clear. At once Succubus leered and let euphoria pierce the blackest of impious hearts.

The Demon Chronicles: The Beauty that is Naamah

Lupita Morales strolled into a small gas station and made her way toward a counter that was enveloped by a newly installed shield made of bullet-resistant glass. Central Avenue was a tough place, one well known for prostitution and drug dealing. Even at a little past midnight the avenue was jumping, the four-lane blacktop littered with cruisers and hunters searching for some tush and push.

At the counter stood a young blonde woman dressed in a blouse and jeans. As she turned to leave, she spotted Lupita and gasped, well-manicured hands thrown up in mock defense. Lupita pushed back several tresses of black hair from her forehead and pressed forward, her eyes made of stone. The young woman smiled, but it was too late—the damage was done. She tucked tail and walked out the door.

A young man behind the counter closed the cash register and sat on a round stool. He was about to pick up a textbook and a green highlighter pen when he spotted the disfigured brunette.

"Hey Lepeeta," he said, trampling all over her name. "Busy tonight?"

"Little bit. Same with you, I gather."

"Not too bad." The boy adjusted his glasses and looked beyond the girl. "Sort of like you, I guess. Mostly coming in spurts."

Lupita had grown accustomed to aversion. In her world there existed two types of people: those who gawked and those who looked away. It had been only two years since the incident and yet she had aged considerably since that time. She felt like an old soul, her aura an amalgamation of filigree at the center of which resided a heavily wrinkled spider. Life would never be the same.

Five years ago, Lupita was a senior in high school, active mostly in theater and cheerleading. She had wanted to become an actress, and upon graduation, she drove an old Volkswagen bus to Hollywood, which two years later spit her out like a rotten tooth. Then she worked as a waitress and later helped out at a warehouse, where she met Doug Stone. He introduced her to the lucrative world of pornography and prostitution.

At first, her looks attracted numerous Johns each night, but alcohol, drugs, and abuse soon took their toll. When she could no longer cut it in Hollywood, Stone shipped her to New Mexico, where she walked the "track" and every once in a while was offered a porno role or other "special" assignment.

Lupita had been working the track when her life changed forever. A drunken john picked her up at about three o'clock in the morning. The sot gave her a twenty for a blowjob. When he popped, the bastard held her down on his lap, forcing his lukewarm jism into her mouth. Despite the john's strength, Lupita managed to pull away. Angry, she spat the cum in his face. His response had been quick and decisive: he used a straight razor to slice her face in half. The strike cut her from the top edge of her left eyebrow down her eye, part of her cheek, lips, and chin. The fucker then threw her out of the late-model Dodge truck and left her for dead.

"Listen, 'Flaco,' I need a favor." Lupita smiled, the scar on her face disappearing from her lips for the moment. "Bathroom key, please."

"Anything but that, hon—you know I just can't do it no more. Listen, the vice boys was here several times tonight. I think they've sniffed out the filthy rubbers in that there little girl's room, darling. They're on to you."

"Come on, Flaco, just one more time. For me?"

"Oh hell, Lepeeta." Flaco picked up a key attached to a large piece of metal and handed it over.

"Don't take too long now. And don't leave a fucking mess this time—pick up them filthy rubbers and at least flush them down the commode!"

"I'll pop him fast." Lupita opened her mouth and flicked her tongue like a nervous serpent.

Lupita stepped into the night. A warm wind caressed her exposed belly and legs as she stood in front of a tall, middle-aged man dressed in a business suit.

"Got the key, mister," she said, holding the metal bar as if it were a trophy.

"You sure it's safe?" his voice boomed.

"It's cool, baby. Come on."

The couple stepped into the bathroom. Lupita locked the door behind them while the gray-haired man leaned against a counter.

"Where are all the girls tonight?" he asked.

"It's Friday night, mister. Busy night for all of us."

"Figured as much. So, ten dollars is what we agreed to, correct?"

She nodded.

"Good."

Dropping her knees onto a cold concrete floor, Lupita zipped down the man's trousers and pulled out a sizable member, which she swallowed quickly to the hilt. The john groaned hard several times as Lupita withdrew the cock, pushed it upward, and used her tongue to flick at the helmet's split.

"God damn, woman," he snarled between clenched teeth.

Lupita turned her head to one side and spit a thick glob of jism onto the concrete floor. The john was far from finished, however. He dug gnarled fingers into thick tresses of obsidian hair and pulled her toward his pulsing cock once again. As he relinquished a fresh load, he used her nose, cheeks, and lips like a napkin to wipe himself clean. With a final groan he released her. Lupita stood up and tugged at the paper-towel dispenser. It was empty.

"Not bad, baby," the green-eyed man muttered as he tugged at the cock protruding from a pair of well-pressed trousers. "I have to admit I was going to pass you by back there. I'm sure glad I didn't."

"Don't like ugly girls?" Lupita turned on a faucet and splashed cold water onto her face.

The john turned around and stared at a mirror, which was cracked in several places, multiplying their faces at least tenfold. Lupita had reached into a black purse for some makeup and lipstick, which she layered on to cover up the scar as best she could.

"I didn't mean it to come off like that, darling. It's just—well, you've got one hell of a package there." The john slapped her tight fanny. "Pity someone carved on you like that. Ever think of having a doctor fix you up? Shit, any number of plastic surgeons could make that face right again."

"I'm saving for it right now," she sneered.

"Money," he grunted as he tucked his cock into his pants. "I'm fucking up left and right tonight. Seriously, doll, I am so

41

sorry. I've reached an age where I just speak my mind is all. Maybe I should just shut the fuck up."

Lupita extended a hand, palm up and fingers slightly curled. The john grinned, took out a wallet, and dropped two twenty-dollar bills on the counter.

"I'll look for you again," he said looking away. "Thank you."

The door slammed, its reverberations resonating for an eternity while Lupita contemplated her face in the cracked mirror. She dropped to her knees, letting her forehead rest on the counter. One of the faucets began dripping, the drops cascading off the metal bowl. The sound soon was replaced with uncontrollable sobs. As she tried hard to regain control of her emotions, the door slammed again.

"Flaco?"

Lupita looked up. The cracks of the mirror had disappeared. In the reconstituted glass floated a pair of piercing red eyes. The young woman stood up and whirled around, but she found that she was still alone. She turned back to the mirror, where the eyes remained, their pupils focused on her. Buzz-like whispers tickled the outer range of her hearing and the taint of brimstone lingered in otherwise stagnant air.

"*Dios mio*," she whispered.

"There is no God here." The voice resonated through the bathroom, ebbing and flowing like a gentle wind through broken reeds. "Do not avert your eyes! Look at me."

Euphoria rushed through the wide-eyed girl. Deep inside she wanted to embrace the source of those eyes and yet she could not understand why. She placed the palms of her hands on the counter to steady herself. The bathroom's lights flickered and one of the toilets flushed and flushed until water seeped from its filth-crusted bowl.

Taking a deep breath, Lupita looked up and stared into the mirror. The eyes were gone and the cracks along the glass had returned. The lavatory's overhead lights sizzled with intensity, revealing what Lupita knew all too well. Even through the makeup she could see the gray circles around her eyes, the cuts and bruises about her skin, and cracked and dry lips. The scar was only one facet of her perceived ugliness. Her hard life had given her the countenance of an old crone.

"Do you like what you see?" the voice asked, its pitch high and its cadence mesmerizing.

"No," Lupita answered, a fingernail removing a crusty from her right eye. "But there is nothing I can do."

"There is a way," the voice beckoned. "But the path is easy and unforgiving."

"Who are you? What do you want?"

A thin layer of mist spread across the mirror, its vacuous tentacles erasing the cracks on the glass for a second time. At the mirror's apex there appeared a wondrous face, one filled with youth and vitality. At first Lupita did not recognize the visage as her own, but as the mist cleared she realized the image was of her idealized self.

"Why do you torment me so?" she asked as tears flowed once more. "I have suffered enough!"

"This is the beauty of Naamah," the voice continued without concern or rancor. "If you wish it, reach out and take it."

"No! This is a lie. It's a lie!"

"Take it, girl. A whore requires beauty, not dignity. Relinquish the latter and embrace the sins of vanity, lust, and sloth. Forsake the dust, for you are made of filth and sediment, much like the sister that imbues those who forsake the second one, who many call Eve."

"I am a whore!" Lupita screamed at the mirror. "I am a whore!"

"Then strike now, harlot! Strike now and make yours the beauty of Naamah."

Lupita slapped her right palm into the mirror with such force that the glass shattered, its shards dispersing all over the lavatory's counter and floor. The poor girl ran screaming into the street.

"Run, whore of Jerusalem!" the voice cackled. "Run!"

~ ~ ~ ~ ~ ~ ~ ~

Bestowed with the beauty of Naamah, Lupita Morales on the following evening walked the track for less than two hours. In such a short time she attracted no less than ten benefactors, all of whom requested half and half, shorthand for a quick suck to get the juices flowing followed by a missionary fuck. In times past, Lupita would have charged thirty dollars for such services, but with her revitalized looks, she upped the price to eighty dollars. Of the ten clients, six were so impressed they also tipped generously.

For the next four months Lupita walked the track, strengthening the number of steady customers willing to pay her exorbitant rate of $150 for either half and half or straight sex. Several men asked if they could set up discrete appointments, something she had never done before. At first Lupita was hesitant, but with her new income she rented a house and purchased a cell phone. She soon found it was no longer necessary to walk the streets, for the phone calls outweighed her steady street clientele.

The men in her stable began passing her phone number on to other interested parties, including several women who were too shy to seek out such services in public. Several prominent businessmen and even some politicians also began soliciting her charms. Lupita moved into a townhouse far away from the track and worked exclusively from home.

Lupita's newly acquired wealth brought with it one principal vice. Fortunately, alcohol and drugs were not an issue, as she had disdained both because she had seen so many of her friends relinquish their souls to such demons to become despondent addicts. No, Lupita's vice was jewelry, and lots of it. She had no reason for the vice—it seemed to have blossomed soon after her encounter with the sanguine eyes. Rings, bracelets, earrings, necklaces, and even pierced jewelry became obsessions. The trinkets were so superfluous that she literally jingled when she walked.

And so it was that Lupita jingled her way through the lobby of the La Fonda hotel in Santa Fe, New Mexico's longstanding capital city. After a brief stop at the front desk, she strolled past the pool and knocked on the door of one of the high-priced bungalows. Moments later, the door opened and she waltzed inside.

Before she could even get comfortable, two men grabbed her arms and dragged her past a couch. While a third man tossed aside papers and knickknacks on a wooden desk, the other two men stripped off her jacket, blouse, and bra. The couple then slammed her face first onto the desk, her breasts slapping the writing table's lacquered surface.

Held down, Lupita tried to relax. It was obvious the fucker who had paid close to $500 for her wanted a rough-play or humiliation scenario. As long as things did not get out of hand, she was game. Besides, the two goons knew better than to remove her jewelry, so she was convinced that they had been briefed.

45

A pair of smooth hands pulled down her skirt and panties. Cold palms rubbed each cheek then spanked it, the taut flesh quivering only slightly.

"Impressive," came a voice. "My type, exactly."

Lupita had heard the voice before. She could not be certain, but it sounded like Governor Choo Choo Torres. Her suspicions were confirmed when she felt the man lift his prodigious gut upward as he eased his pelvis onto her butt. Cigarette breath blasted the side of her face and the man leaned onto her, his weight making it difficult for her to suspire.

"I want to show these boys how we do it out here in New Mexico, okay?"

"Sure thing, cowboy."

Thick fingers parted her cheeks wide as the governor shoved his cock not into her slit but into her tight, star-shaped button. Lupita groaned as Torres crammed a short but thick slab of sausage to its hilt, his fat ass grinding as he let loose with a series of half-assed thrusts. Not satisfied with just piercing her forbidden hole, Torres bumped against her several more times, keeping his cock inside her while he ejaculated. Globs of off-brown juice trickled down the girl's legs as he withdrew.

"Get her the fuck out of here!" he bellowed, reaching for a towel draped over a nearby couch. "And Solomon, make sure it was worth her while. Understand?"

While the governor and several of his aides vacated the room to attend a nearby luncheon for a powerful senator, the man Torres had called Solomon waited for Lupita to get dressed. It was slow going, for her ass had been torn in two. She stumbled to retrieve a towel and then struggled with her undergarments and blouse. Solomon was not impressed. Rather, he stood by the door and lit a cigarette, all the time his slit eyes admiring the Latina's wares.

"Lupe, how much for a boy like me?" Solomon grasped the bulge in his trousers. "How about a discount for the workingman?"

"You can't even afford the discount rate, *chulito*."

"*Aye caramba*," he exhaled. "Thing is, I know what you like, *chica*. Take a minute and see what I got hanging down here."

Intrigued but still sore, Lupita put her hands on her hips and grinned. "I've seen them all, stud. What does yours have that others don't?"

Solomon squared his hips and pulled down his zipper. Chomping on the cigarette in his nicotine-saturated mouth, he used both hands to whip out a mediocre cock. Solomon was right, however. He knew well what Lupita loved above everything else. Hanging around his cock, decorating the man's fat nutsac, was a silver necklace that ended with a simple pearl.

"You want it?" Solomon asked with a wry grin.

"Yes." Lupita licked her lips. "I want it."

"Come and get it then." Solomon flicked his middle finger off his cock's bulbous helmet. "One thing, though. This pearl is very special. I want you to remove all your jewelry before you claim it."

"You want me to take off my jewels? Fuck you!"

"Have it your way." Solomon shrugged. "You need understand, however, that this pearl was worn exclusively by virgins. Any type of jewelry would ruin its innate powers. I'm not asking for a fuck or suck. Just strip down, walk over, and take it."

Lupita nodded. She began by slowly removing her blouse, pushing her elbows down to get out of the sleeves and then lifting it over her head. As the fine fabric floated toward the carpeted floor, she unfastened her bra, which she also let fall to the floor. After removing her heels, she let drop her skirt and then eased out of her panties.

Naked, Lupita took a step forward, her jewelry jingling and jangling. With another step she removed her diamond necklace. Two more steps and she took off her bracelets and watch. Three more steps and off came two-dozen rings of all shapes and sizes. She then stopped, bent down, and removed several anklets.

Solomon was impressed. He used both hands to tug at his cock, and as the woman discarded a nose stud, he ejaculated, trickles of diluted juice splotching onto the carpet.

"Like a strip show, do you?" Lupita winked.

"No," Solomon responded almost instantly. "I like what happens next."

Close enough to claim her prize, Lupita dropped to her knees. As she did so, however, her legs buckled and she fell to one side. She extended an arm to right herself, but this appendage also failed her. Panicked, she tried to roll off her back but found she lacked the strength to move. Solomon hovered above her, the pearl necklace still dangling from his lackluster member.

"Come, my child. Come and claim your prize."

Lupita looked up. From out of Solomon's chiseled face stared a pair of piercing red eyes. The eyes were not his; they belonged to another, for their facets were uniquely feminine. Gathering the last of her strength, Lupita made to stand. As she did so, her left leg and right arm snapped off like twigs from a dead tree. As she fell onto her belly, her remaining appendages came off as well. The poor girl slithered like a snake, her head moving from side to side.

~ ~ ~ ~ ~ ~ ~ ~

Sitting on a throne carved of obsidian and ebony, Crimson Succubus looked down at her latest acquisition. The young woman looked so beautiful, the scar across her face sending ripples through the she-devil's swollen clit, which the she played like a harp. Lupita's armless and legless trunk had been placed on a pedestal with specially designed metal clamps that held her upright.

Lupita opened her eyes and noticed the winged demon. Sobbing, she surveyed her surroundings. As best she could determine, she was in a deep cavern of some sort, for all about her were strange rock formations made even more hideous by the multitude of shadows that gave them a bizarre type of dark luminescence. She made to stand but then realized her nightmare was far from over; her arms and legs were gone. Lupita remained as cursed as the Nagas, whose tasks according to ancient Indian myths included guarding precious jewels or other treasure.

"Your eyes," Lupita whimpered. "I know your eyes."

"Do you now?" Succubus stood up and spread her wings. "You have come to me at last, whore of Jerusalem. I shall honor you always."

Succubus stood in front of the half-woman. She placed a claw upon Lupita's face.

"I give you back the beauty of Naamah, which you have earned. And with it shall you have bestowed upon you the worship you have craved so much during your wretched existence. Come, my children. Come and partake of the Jezebel."

From the deepest recesses of the cave emerged hideous imps whose ebon skin released thick clouds of sable smoke. Although each abomination had its own particular attributes, most were no more than half the size of their mistress. Their conical heads were hairless and their faces were expressionless. Two slit eyes centered a bulbous nose, below which was a pair of thick lips. Their bodies were short and consisted of broad shoulders, thick arms, pudgy hands, wide torsos, and squat legs.

Lupita could not help but stare at their sex, which came as a surprise. Despite the lack of breasts, the things were undoubtedly female.

One of the more adventurous imps stepped forward and extended a furtive hand. Thin fingers ending with curled spurs clasped one of Lupita's breasts. The imp did not rip or shred it, but rather the creature weighed it in her palm like the Egyptian god Thoth weighed a heart upon the scales of justice. The thing hissed and advanced, ravenous lips parting to expose a forked tongue.

"Whore!" the imp screeched before wrapping its maw around Lupita's breast.

Having seen their sister succumb to lechery, the other imps joined the frenzy, their claws and tongues partaking of the half-woman's honey-sweet flesh.

Succubus returned to her throne, from which she witnessed the assault upon the whore of Jerusalem. The Latin girl looked like a massive phallus, her glistening skin worshipped by the next generation of Lilim who one day would leave the Red Sea and lay siege to the earth and heavens.

Engulfed by the throng, Lupita could do nothing but scream, the resonance of her shrieks serving as the seed of hell itself.

Branding Nina

Five of Crimson Succubus's strongest thralls dragged the Nubian Nina toward a red-hot forge. Upon a massive anvil they chained the obstinate woman, who even now screamed at the top of her lungs.

Succubus stood by a steaming hearth, the flames lapping at her leathery wings and tail. She picked up a rod and placed its end into the kiln. In that hideous maw of red and white she rotated it round and round.

"Begin, my thralls," she ordered.

With her command given, the men lowered their trousers and held high their long, thick cocks. Strong, callused hands worked the shafts' length while index fingers teased bloated, mushroom-like heads. Groans filled the air, blending with Nina's insistent screams, and in that cacophony Succubus opened her wings to absorb all the calenture and consternation that would come her way.

"Behind me, thralls," she ordered as she retrieved the rod and walked over to Nina. "Be still, my slave."

The brand hissed on ebony flesh, Succubus's mark forever etched upon the canvass of Nina's skin. Succubus stepped back, her hands releasing the rod. Arching her back, she allowed her fingernails to migrate toward the slit between her epicurean thighs.

"Now!"

The thralls stepped forward, shooting wave after wave of silver juice onto Nina's face and neck. Succubus then moved forward, pushing the thralls aside. The demon fell to her knees and extended a long, snake-like tongue. With uncanny precision she licked along the outline of the indelible mark.

"You are mine now," she whispered.

"Thank you, Mistress," responded the slave before passing out.

Shackled in Perpetuity

Crimson Succubus squatted before her thrall, the lovely Nubian Nina. In an open palm dangled a pair of iron manacles, fire-treated so the metal was strong and smooth. Succubus placed a cheek against Nina's stomach. Bringing her free hand around to cup the thrall's ample but supple bottom, Succubus drew her closer, the she-devil's flesh burning Nina's mahogany skin. The slave gasped; in response, Succubus moved her cheek downward, at last easing it into the moist and tender crevice between well-muscled thighs.

Looking down, Nina licked her lips, smacking them as Succubus began twisting the manacles from side to side. The thrall arched her back, and as her arms floated upward, the sweat lining her midsection constricted in intricate patterns. Succubus turned her face inward, her lips resting against Nina's cleft.

"Oh, Mistress!"

Succubus pulled away and grinned. Before Nina could react, the she-devil snapped the manacles around the thrall's ankles. She then stood up and reached for another pair. Nina stared at the irons. They were simple shackles, well constructed with burnished bolts and what appeared to be a complex locking mechanism. The chain between the anklets allowed her to stand akimbo but no more. She surmised that she could hobble but walking would present a problem.

"Extend your arms and interlace your fingers."

The suddenness of Succubus's command startled Nina, so much so that as she obeyed she also lifted her eyes, locking them temporarily on those burning orbs of her mistress. As Succubus placed the armlets onto Nina's wrists, taking notice of the moment of indiscretion, and once the irons were secure, she withdrew several steps and brought her open hand back.

"Forgive!" Nina begged.

The backhand almost took Nina to the ground, but she managed to stabilize her sweat-lined thighs and tighten her wondrous gut. Succubus's eyes continued to blaze—their enflamed orbs scintillating like blood on glass—but rather than strike again, the she-devil stepped forward and spread her leathery wings, which in turn engulfed most of Nina's slender body.

"Remain still, darling," Succubus whispered.

From the she-devil's pliant lips emerged a long, trident-tipped tongue. The asp-like appendage extended forward, at length coming into contact with Nina's lower lip. There, the lingua fluttered like a butterfly in flight, its tip wiping away several droplets of blood that had collected at the mouth's edge. Nina fought to keep her own tongue in check.

"Delicate creature," Succubus crooned as she smacked her lips.

Into the alcove entered four brawny thralls. Two-by-two, the men carried a massive hearth between them, the conveyance poles bending from its cumbrous weight. Sweating profusely, the thralls placed the hearth in front of Nina and then closed a massive iron door behind them.

Succubus stood across from the hearth, staring at its crackling coals. With silent elegance she reached for a poker, which even now glowed red from intense heat. Nina blinked her downcast eyes. When she had first come under the demon's service, she underwent an intricate branding ritual. Was she to change owners?

"No branding for you, darling," Succubus said as if responding to the slave's very thoughts. "At least not one of ownership. Something different, I would think."

As Nina sat on her calves, Succubus began stirring the hearth's contents, making the flames go higher and higher while the embers sparked and hissed. Driving the rod deep into the emulsion, she twisted it round and round, bringing out other colors, such as bright blue, scintillating yellow, and gelatinous black. Smoke began filling the tiny room.

"Remain here. Do not change position. Wait for me."

With that, Succubus withdrew.

~ ~ ~ ~ ~ ~ ~ ~

For uncounted hours Nina knelt before a hearth, her wrists and ankles manacled. At first she rather enjoyed the bonds, particularly the ones on her wrists. The iron felt cold, but as time passed, she felt the metal become one with her body's heat. She kept her forearms extended, making a game out of the shackles' ballast. Sometime later, she abandoned the diversion, bringing her hands to her stomach, but even then she could not escape their weight. Sweating profusely, the slave ached for their removal, so she began fidgeting, and at once she felt the weight of the anklets, the tops of which were digging into flesh and bone. The discomfort was not altogether intolerable, but it was enough for her to remain alert. Perhaps that was what her mistress had in mind—she would not disappoint her.

At twilight, the iron door opened and into the room stepped Lord Draco, one of the Succubus's overseers. Tall and muscular, the man was dressed like an executioner, his face obscured by a leather cowl from which escaped tresses of waist-length hair. Two suicide straps were wrapped around his chest, holding up a pair of loose-fitting synthetic pants lined with infinite rhinestones. On his forearms he wore spiked bracelets.

Without fanfare Draco dropped to one knee and removed the anklets. As he did so, Nina placed her head on his shoulder, letting her hair tease his nose.

"Lord," she sighed licking her tongue. "Now the shackles about my wrists, in exchange for any favor. Please, let me rest, if only for a moment. I have talents you must experience, my lord."

Draco stood up and placed a boot on Nina's left thigh. He then grabbed her wrists and produced a silver key. Nina began writhing like a snake expecting a meal, but instead of removing the wrist-irons, Draco tightened them, cutting off much of the circulation in her tingling and numb hands.

"Lord?"

Draco clasped Nina's neck with his left hand, while with his right he unbuttoned his trousers.

"The favor," he growled.

Eyes downcast, Nina reached out and lowered the man's pants, causing a thick cock to spring out, its mushroom head bouncing up and down. Before Nina could reach for his love-member, Draco pulled her in, squeezing her neck so that her mouth opened wide. As she struggled to breathe, Draco used one hand to clasp the cock by its base. He then shoved its length into her, driving it all the way down her throat. There he kept it for a moment or two, and as he withdrew ever so slowly, he shot a glutinous load, the alabaster fluid dribbling down the sides of her mouth.

"No water, so drink up."

With a snarl he relinquished his hold on her. He then took his cock and wiped the dregs on her shoulder and breasts.

"These, I'll keep." He rattled the ankle manacles.

"Don't leave me, Lord!"

"Be still. She soon shall be with you again."

And with that he left the room.

~ ~ ~ ~ ~ ~ ~ ~

At dawn, the succubus known as Sable Agrate—a powerful and malevolent Lilim in her own right—walked into the small chamber and found Nina asleep, although she remained on her knees. As quietly as possible, the she-devil walked over to the girl and watched as her breasts moved to the rhythm of blissful slumber. Bringing her ebon wings into the back of her body, Agrate sat down and crossed her legs like a Buddha preparing for meditation. She then reached for the girl's left ankle, which she began massaging with unusually long fingers, the ends of which looked like exaggerated spurs.

With a start Nina opened her eyes. Her first instinct was to run, but she knew well that if she moved, Crimson Succubus would enact an even more severe form of punishment. So instead she took several spasmodic breaths, and as she did so she came to realize someone was massaging one of her heavily bruised feet.

"Poor little beast," whispered Agrate, her talons rubbing Nina's swollen toes. "My sanguine-skinned sister is far too cruel, what with her notion that discipline and lust must be one and the same. Wantonness should be expressed freely, not with so much hubbub and crude accouterments. What do you think, dearest?"

Nina trembled, shivers coating her whole body. Agrate's words tasted like fine wine, and at a perfunctory level she let them intoxicate her soul. But deep inside Nina accepted Crimson Succubus as her one and only mistress. She wore the demon's brand on her neck. It was the sign of a fine heard. She was Galatea to Pygmalion, for Succubus had molded her from lifeless ebony into a creature made of flesh and bone. Without her mistress she was nothing, and it was also true that without her the she-devil was nothing. They were yin and yang, dragon and tiger, black and silver. And so it was that Nina remained silent while the she-devil continued massaging her ticklish foot.

Bored, Agrate gently put down the thrall's ankle, cracked her knuckles by twisting her wrist several times, and locked her unusually long hand around Nina's chin. With her free hand she clasped the slave's right wrist, easing her middle finger under the shackles so it pricked at the flesh beneath.

"Answer me."

The talon dug into the flesh. Several drops of blood emerged, one of them dropping onto the stone floor. There it spattered, creating a wondrously decadent pattern. Agrate admired the stain but soon turned her attention back to Nina. Squeezing her chin, she forced the poor girl to look into her eyes.

"I will not ask again, little one: answer me."

With her talons dug deep into Nina's chin, Agrate pulled her forward. While she licked Nina's lips, the demon ran her middle finger along the girl's wrist, creating a tiny gash that quickly filled with blood. Standing up, Agrate wrenched Nina's wrists over the hearth. Several drops of blood fell onto the coals. Smoke turned pitch black as the viscous fluid sizzled on fiery rocks.

Agrate pushed down, easing the girl's arms closer to the flames. Heat coated tender forearms with a nice shade of red; tiny hairs curled at the intense tepidity. Gooseflesh formed about Nina's forehead and shoulders, turning curiously cold as she began shivering. She wanted very much to scream and run, but she held firm, her quivers becoming inextricable spasms of anticipation as Agrate pushed the arms even lower. Covered with perspiration, Nina closed her eyes, calmed her breath, and waited.

"It seems I have my answer."

Agrate set the thrall loose, leaving the wrist shackles on, and exited the chamber.

~ ~ ~ ~ ~ ~ ~ ~

At midday, Nina's precious knees were covered with welts. She had been stalwart in her efforts to remain motionless, at most moving her arms up and down to keep the flesh from tingling or arching her shoulders to relieve some of the pressure on her lower back and thighs. When the door opened, Nina held her breath. She was certain that yet another of her mistress's minions would enter and like a feline treat her like a ball of string.

Rays from the sun streaking about her cerise body, Crimson Succubus stood in the entryway. She inspected her thrall, folded her wings, and snapped her tail before walking into the room. Once inside, she dropped to one knee and scrutinized Nina, focusing the majority of her attention on Nina's wrists and the manacles that remained fixed and secure.

"Spurned all propositions, I see."

The she-devil brought her tail around and forced the barbed tip between the iron cuffs and Nina's burning flesh. When Succubus rubbed the tail on the delicate skin, Nina gasped, her back stiffening and her eyes growing wide. It took everything she had left to stifle a shriek.

"Very good."

"Thank you, Mistress," Nina said, smirking with relief.

"Don't thank me yet, dear."

Succubus used her statuesque thighs to push herself up; concurrently, she reached out with her left hand and clasped Nina's manacles. As she stood up, she also wrenched the thrall upward. Succubus took several furtive steps back, carefully moving around the still-burning hearth. She then pulled Nina's arms over the cauldron-shaped vessel and without any forewarning brought the shackles in direct contact with the fiery coals.

Nina screamed as the shackles seethed from the heat. The iron radiated torridity, its emanations like lice jumping onto Nina's already damaged flesh. Nina felt her legs buckle, but she knew if she fell the top of her body would succumb to the same fiery fate. So instead she used her upper canines and incisors to dig into her lower lip, immediately drawing forth so much blood that the thick fluid dripped down her chin, over her engorged breasts, and onto the floor.

Succubus's impious heart rejoiced as Nina at last passed out from the pain. The demon released her hold and allowed the thrall to fall to one side. Nina had assimilated so much of the hearth's heat that the coals had grown lukewarm, with the rocks on the periphery of the black cauldron actually having grown cold.

"Wake up, beloved," Succubus said, dropping to one knee. She then used a curved fingernail to tap Nina's face gently. "It is time to resume your duties."

Nina sat up. Succubus produced an elaborately carved passe-partout and removed the shackles, letting them drop onto the ground. The thrall rubbed her wrists, which had been permanently scarred from the manacles. The irons' outline was perpetually etched into her skin. The thrall's eyes widened as she admired the unique tattoos.

"Oh, thank you, Mistress!" Nina blurted out.

Succubus beamed and hugged her thrall. "Back to your chores, cherished one. And you are quite welcome, Nina. You have more than earned this honor."

For two cycles of moons Nina continued to admire her immutable shackles, taking particular pleasure when she would wash her hands or when she was allowed to wear jewelry that accented her wrists.

Months later, during a particularly brutal snowstorm, Nina was tidying up the Sanguinary Parlor in Succubus's citadel when she heard steps behind her. She dropped to her knees and averted her gaze, staring at the carpet. Into the room walked Crimson Succubus, a pair of ankle irons cradled in her left arm.

As Succubus began her tease-lecture, Nina felt an orgasm already building deep inside. Many more would come as her ankles were subjected to the loving ways of Crimson Succubus.

Seven Gold Coins for Shana

A middle-aged man stood in a modestly adorned parlor. Tired of waiting, he stiffened his back as his beady eyes darted back and forth and a quivering slit of a mouth whispered prayers of resoluteness and self-induced chastity. In his hands the esquire clutched a worn Bible.

He was no priest, nor was he even given to any of theology's trappings, but black thoughts had clouded his head for many months, thoughts he had found flagrantly stimulating, at times even strangely titillating. Although he was here, deep inside he wished to flee the brothel. A battle of wills had begun within him, and for the moment licentiousness domineered dogma.

A door eased shut, its click bringing the man back from a fervent and self-induced malaise. Having assumed the guise of a human woman, Crimson Succubus walked into the sitting room, the bustle of her flowing scarlet gown moving from side to side. The Bible still clutched in both hands, the middle-aged gentleman turned and stared at the woman. She wore her raven hair loose, its tresses teasing slightly red skin. Two sanguine eyes stared into his, and in that instant her slit-like lips parted and a long, wickedly shaped tongue licked her lower labrum.

A sable corset was wrapped about her slender frame, the bodice lifting full breasts, their nipples stretching the fabric that held them in check. She sat on an overstuffed couch, and as she crossed her legs she exposed a pair of finely woven stockings that encased muscular thighs and well-contoured calves. Her feet were small, the stiletto heels wrapped around them twice the average length.

"Marcus, isn't it?" she hissed, her voice like a cobra, its cadence quick and lethal.

"Yes, madam."

Succubus smiled, patting a cushion on the couch. "Entertain me for a moment."

Marcus sat down, placing the holy book between them.

"A man of letters, are you?" Succubus licked her upper lip then made to switch thighs, a nectar-like perfume escaping from between them as she kicked one leg over the other.

"Yes," he responded with a nod. "I—" He stared at the ceiling and watched as a fan went round and round. "That is to say," he stammered yet again. "I mean—"

"You have a special request?"

"Shana," he blurted.

Succubus laughed, covering her mouth but recovering quickly.

Marcus stiffened. "Shana," he repeated, this time with more assurance.

"Of course, Marcus. Ours is to please." Succubus stared at his crotch and smiled at the bulge burgeoning there. "Seven gold coins and she is yours for the night."

"She is here, then?"

"Oh yes, dear Marcus. She knew you would come. She always knows."

Marcus placed seven gold coins in Succubus's outstretched hand. As he pulled back, the she-devil teased the man's ring finger, around which was a platinum wedding band.

"Upstairs," Succubus waved him away.

~ ~ ~ ~ ~ ~ ~ ~

Once he stepped into the room, the door closed behind him and several locks slid into place of their own accord.

Marcus took another furtive step in the pitch-black chamber, but then he froze. Several feet away, she was there. He could smell her. Virile musk overlaid with expensive perfume, an intoxicating nectar that belonged exclusively to the creature known as Shana.

Shana lit several candles and then stood across from Marcus, her eyes locked on his. Still clutching the Bible, Marcus let his eyes move downward, past the auburn hair, wide eyes, rustic cheeks, and full lips to a long neck, lithe collarbone, and wide shoulders. Then there was her exposed bosom, each breast full, its aureole beaming red and each nipple almost lavender. A black leather corset pushed up the breasts while adding delicate curvature to the woman's lower torso and stomach.

Stepping back, Shana ran her soft hands down her sides, delicate fingers teasing taut thighs. Between her legs hung eight inches of thick, round meat, with two of these inches dedicated to a mushroom helmet that even now tingled with concupiscence.

"You can touch it, Marcus." Shana smiled. "Mmmmm, you could even lick it."

Marcus shook his head.

Shana stared at his trousers. "Or would you rather that I worship upon your succulent altar?"

Marcus nodded.

On her knees, Shana placed her face on the fabric, her lips finding Marcus's manhood. She bit through the pants, her teeth teasing the member within. Wrapping her hands around his buttocks, she pulled him into her. Saliva stained the fabric, turning it pleasantly darker. While she teased his butt cheeks with her fingers, Shana unbuckled his belt, unbuttoned and unzipped his trousers, and allowed the garment to fall to the floor.

Without hesitation Shana used her left hand to grasp his cock by its base. She squeezed the shaft firmly, turning the tiny mushroom head a dark shade of purple. She flicked at the helmet, her tongue bouncing off flesh only to return again and again. Opening wide, she took him in an inch at a time, concurrently releasing the base and moving her index finger to his balls. Behind them she teased a hidden and mostly forgotten portion of the shaft. Marcus groaned—he had never felt a shiver from inside his cock, but as Shana sucked and teased with her finger, he quaked like a schoolboy just before the paddle stuck fabric and the tingling flesh just underneath.

Marcus clenched his teeth as his cock began to ache. Shana responded by taking him all the way down her throat, saliva lining the sides of her mouth and staining her neck and breasts. The holy book, which he had been clutching in his right hand, fell to the floor, where it landed with a thump. Marcus looked down; Shana's cock was engorged, its wonderful helmet hovering above the book.

Before he could move, Shana twirled her tongue round and round and eased her right hand's middle finger into his chaste button. Marcus groaned as she worked it in and out, with each thrust inward going deeper and deeper, the sphincter abdicating its frail virginity. With both hands he grabbed her auburn hair and with ardent fury slammed his cock in and out of her mouth. Shana wrapped her lips around his cock, her face bobbing as he mouth-fucked her.

As climax consumed him, Shana rubbed her cock, and both of them exploded at the same time. Anemic, pale cum oozed down the sides of her face while thick gobs of cum covered the leather jacket of the holy book, the viscous droplets coalescing upon the embossed outline of a golden cruciform.

Without a word Marcus cleaned himself off, pulled up his trousers and picked up the Bible, dropped several gold coins onto the floor, and made his way to the door. Shana stood up, her hands working her massive member again, the remains of cum oozing out of its impressive head.

"I hope your wife enjoys the smell of that book's leather," she whispered.

Marcus stood at the door a moment. Stiff once again, he opened it, paused, and then stepped out, not once looking back.

Shana sat on a plain wooden chair and continued to work herself. The door creaked open and Crimson Succubus peeked inside.

"You marked his baneful book, dear Shana?"

"Yes, Mistress."

"He'll bring a fresh one tomorrow."

"I understand, Mistress."

"Good. Continue."

The door closed, this time the catches and bolts neutralized. Shana smiled. Poor bastard, she thought. Like God, Lucifer had countless minions, and they likewise worked in mysterious ways.

The Art of Forniphilia

Lady Lydia had ruled Icetock for close to five congregations of a trio of moons. In that time she had come to realize that her stronghold and its megaron were little more than a prison filled with lackluster masonry and baubles, drab tapestries and spoils taken from countless conquests, and a throne so uncomfortable her wondrously curved bottom ached from its adamantine surface. And so it was that she had brought before her that she-devil known as Crimson Succubus. Lady Lydia's decree was simple: "Build me a megaron the likes of which no soul, evanescent or eternal, has ever fathomed. I crave harmony, and harmony I shall have."

Having spilt blood and unfailingly served the Lady Lydia heretofore, Crimson Succubus at first wondered how she would carry out such an eccentric decree. For an entire season she wandered the world, seeking knowledge of architecture and design. Many great sights and textures did she experience, but it was not until she met Wu Feng, a master of Feng Shui, that she realized at last that she had come to the end of her quest.

For three seasons she remained under the Asian's tutelage, learning not only the traditional arts, but also the more obscure humanities, including things such as the restraining of human bodies, the ecstasy of suffering, the sorrow of laughter, the love of objects, and the seduction of the soul.

The she-devil worked alone within the megaron. When it was completed, the guards and wards were removed and Succubus emerged.

Her eyes covered with a velvet blindfold, Lady Lydia was led into the megaron. Upon the veil's removal, the lady was shocked, for the throne room had undergone a dramatic alteration. Her breathing became erratic as she tried to absorb the scene before her. At her side was Crimson Succubus, whose slit-like smirk masked feelings of personal achievement.

Gone was the platinum and diamond-encrusted chandelier, in its place a candelabrum made of living flesh. Shackled to a framework made of iron and plated with silver were four albino women, each on their back, their legs pointed upward and feet clamped to steel chains suspended from the ceiling. Each unclothed female held two amber candles, the wax dripping onto their forearms and breasts.

Lady Lydia's throne had been replaced with Nubian men and women dressed from head to toe in crimson leather and hints of ringmail. Two muscular males knelt on one knee, their heads bowed and arms extended and interlocked. Upon their broad shoulders rested two females, bent at the waist, with thighs on their torsos and calves up as a backboard. Resting on the women's thighs and calves were magenta cushions stuffed with the down of a thousand sanctified birds.

And then there was the offering table. At its center, sticking out, was the head of a man, a motley cowl covering his countenance. Turning slowly like a top winding down, the head stared into space. On the top of his crown rested a thick green candle. Surrounding the head were a number of disembodied hands, female, their nails long and decorated with intricate illustrations. Some of the hands held gold and silver coins, others jewelry, and still others were empty, their palms aching to be filled.

"What is this?" Lady Lydia exclaimed.

"I call it forniphilia."

"And this forniphilia is?"

"It is a combination of the Old French word *furnir*, which means 'to furnish,' and the Greek word *philos*, which means 'love of.' Therefore, forniphilia is 'the love of furnishing.'"

"Tell me, she-demon, where is the harmony in this obscene exhibition?"

Succubus waved her left hand. At once the furniture began to sing.

A Night with a Vampire

It had been the intricately carved crucifix made of platinum and tiny multicolored gems that first caught the eye of the she-devil. The cruciform reminded her of times past, when she had beguiled vicars and monks late at night, copulating with them until their seed trickled onto their vow of celibacy. The seductions had become so prevalent that the Vatican instructed the poor self-professed celibates to attach rosaries to their members in a feeble attempt to ward off her nocturnal defilement.

But the sleeper before her was no monk. Indeed, the she-devil was in the presence of a fellow woman. Whether she walked under the eyes of the Dark Lord, Crimson Succubus could not tell. But the trinket hinted at either faith or frolic—Succubus was keen to find out which.

Succubus broke her gaze away from the symbol of piety and looked up. To her surprise she found the wearer staring right at her, the woman's eyes scintillating with a mixture of seduction and beguilement. Succubus sneered, her human countenance for the moment turning almost unsightly as her lips went crooked and her eyes narrowed.

The woman closed her eyes, long lashes teasing soft flesh, and turned around, shifting her weight from one side to the other. Succubus grinned; this one played the game well.

"Greetings," the she-devil whispered from behind, her pointed breasts digging into the female's curved back. "Enjoying yourself?"

The other turned around, the sable bangs from her short, stylish queue bouncing off a slightly protruding forehead. "I am now."

"They call me Lilim."

"Is that so?" She chuckled, her mouth exposing a set of shark-like teeth only for a moment. "I am Katrina." She extended a well-manicured hand, each fingernail decorated with scenes taken from the Catholic Bible and the Egyptian Book of the Dead.

Succubus squeezed the appendage, and as she did so, Katrina moved forward, her free hand wrapping around the demon's lower thigh. Soft as velvet yet cold as permafrost, the palm sent lascivious sensations through the night hag. It was a rare sensation indeed, for she was accustomed to imbuing lust, not receiving it.

"Come with me," Katrina said, her eyes looking upward. "There is a special sanctuary that should appeal to you."

"I am honored."

After entering a lift and quietly ascending to the top floor, the women set foot into a massive penthouse with a singular piece of furniture at its apex: a bed. But this was no ordinary bedstead, for the frame was made of human thralls. Covered from head to toe in glistening latex, a dozen male slaves were bent at the waist, their brawny backs and sinewy thighs supporting a massive mattress. The headboard consisted of two females wearing scarlet cowls, corsets, and thigh-boots.

"An exquisite chamber," muttered Succubus.

"A hobby of mine," Katrina said, removing her flimsy black dress. "It is called forniphilia."

"And it is?"

"It is a combination of the Old French word *furnir*, which means 'to furnish,' and the Greek word *philos*, which means 'love of.' Therefore, forniphilia is 'the love of furnishing.'"

Succubus discarded her red blouse and obsidian pants, revealing a blood-colored corset, a garter belt, and spider-like stockings. Katrina licked her lips as she crawled onto the bed, her thin fingers gently pushing away the satin sheets. Without hesitation Succubus joined her.

"Please," Katrina broke the silence. "Let me see you—I mean, your true countenance. I beg this one indulgence of you."

Succubus frowned.

Nodding, Katrina opened her mouth wide, exposing a pair of extended incisors and pointed canines. She then looked down, her eyes filled with sanguine fire.

Taking the vampire's cue, Succubus arched her back and bared herself: a pair of thick horns protruded from her head, her flesh became the color of blood, leathery wings sprouted from her back, and a wicked tail grew from her lower spine.

"So, you spoke the truth. You are indeed Lilim, a daughter of Lillith."

Succubus barred a mouthful of razor-sharp teeth. "Indeed."

"I am Katrina, shunned even by Anubis, the Jackal God. I have walked this plane so long that only trees whisper about the days of my death."

The two embraced, Succubus driving her tongue deep into the mouth of the vampire. As fingers danced and palms pressed, Katrina ran her tongue along the demon's neck, biting the collarbone and taking her fill. In turn Succubus ran her fingernails down the blood-fiend's back, drawing forth a dark liquid that stained the alabaster sheets. Her mouth dripping blood, Katrina made her way down, teasing the demon's navel and snipping at her pubic hair.

"Stop, Katrina."

The vampire looked up, a bewildered look upon her face.

"Like all women, I am cursed."

A tear escaped the bloodsucker's eye. "Take me, then."

Succubus folded her wings, pressed the vampire's chest down onto some cushions, and gently parted her taut thighs. "The moon has not cursed you yet, then?"

"The moon shall never bless me, Lilim," Katrina muttered, her eyes downcast. "When I walked as a mortal, I was an avatar of Isis. But I grew arrogant and dared ingest her blood, which is called 'sa.' Isis cursed me for my indecorous action and so I was doomed to walk forever in need of blood yet remain bloodless."

Katrina sat up and turned around the crucifix about her neck. On the reverse side was the Egyptian symbol of ankh, whose yonic loop represented a woman's blossom, the source of sa.

"I know fall without summer. For eternity I shall reap and never sow. I walk among the living and shall never embrace life, nor will I taste of that bitter herb known as death."

From deep inside Succubus ascended ache, and for the first time in her cursed life she felt tears well around her baneful eyes. As the fluid made its way down her cheeks, some of it traced across her lips. There was no purity there, only the brackishness of malfeasance.

"Come, let us sleep," the demon finally managed to say.

"I cannot. There is no sleep. Ever. There are, at times, periods of intense self-hypnotism, but these are rare. And less gratifying, I'm afraid, as time wears on. There is never the peace, the solitude, of slumber."

"Wrap your arms around me." Succubus enfolded her wings around the vampire. "Tonight, we shall rest."

Moments later, both creatures of the night fell into a deep sleep.

~ ~ ~ ~ ~ ~ ~ ~

At dawn, the bed-thralls exited the room, leaving a mattress saturated with blood and a singular ebon rose at its heart. Without even the slightest murmur, the slaves sealed the penthouse and were never heard from again.

In another part of the city, in a cemetery long ago forgotten, stood Crimson Succubus, in her talons a small vial filled with crimson nectar.

"The sa of Katrina," she said taking a drink and managing a most impious grin.

Eternal Mummy

Crimson Succubus knelt before Min, the Egyptian god of fertility. Wearing a crown surmounted by two tall plumes, Min sat upon a throne, his ever-erect cock leaking a white sap similar to a phallic-shaped type of lettuce found only in Akhmim, one of the deity's most important sanctuaries.

"What do you wish of me, Lord?" Succubus asked, her sanguine eyes downcast.

"My avatar Neferet, she has consorted with Isis. This indiscretion is not the first, but rather the latest in the infinite Eye of Horus. She is a nymph, one who cannot be sated even by my wondrous member."

"I understand, Lord."

"My mother would be displeased if I were to place Neferet into the paws of that jackal Anubis, so I wish for you to create within her a paroxysm-inducing torment that will endure as long as fury burns within my heart."

"I must have use of the Eye of Horus, so that I may have foresight."

"So shall it be written, so shall it be done."

~ ~ ~ ~ ~ ~ ~ ~

Crimson Succubus stared at the scene before her; at first it looked like a Wiccan ceremony, but the roles were reversed. Standing in a circle were twelve male thralls, all of whom were brawny, wore only sandals, and possessed cocks as long as a Roman gladius. The slaves were stroking themselves, their vigorous hands tight upon their bloated shafts.

In the middle of the circle stood Neferet. From head to toe she had been immobilized. All she could do was watch the men pleasure themselves, and in some instances the bolder among them gratified each other. Succubus had been most thorough in designing Neferet's paralytic attire.

First, a metal hoop decorated with vibrant colors of glass had been placed around her neck. At the edge of the hoop were several tiny blades that pricked her throat, and as a result she was forced to keep her chin in a most regal position.

Second, her delicate hands had been bound with heavily spun rope made of flax. Intricate knots had been designed to grow tighter with even the slightest hint of a struggle.

Third, she wore a corset made of thick leather and laced with three sets of cross-woven buckskin thongs. Several bone-carved needles were sewn within the bust; if Neferet bent down even in the slightest degree, the needles would jab her breasts.

Fourth, her lower body had been encased in a hobble skirt. Made of leather and so tight about her hips, thighs, and calves that little if any sudation managed to escape, the skirt held her knees together, making it impossible to move in any direction.

And fifth, a pair of dagger-high heels graced her feet, which had been wrapped taut with water-soaked bandages.

"I can bear it no longer!" Neferet exclaimed. "Succubus, let me couple with any of these men. I beg this of you!"

Succubus walked into the circle, knelt before one of the thralls, and teased his cock with her forked tongue. Almost instantly the slave exploded, the alabaster fluid coating the demon's crimson flesh.

"You mean, like that?"

"Yes!"

The she-devil threw her head back and cackled. "There is one man."

"Please!" Saliva filled Neferet's mouth.

"Are you sure, my little nymph?"

"I can bear it no longer. I implore you!"

"There is no need to beg. I shall have a servant fetch him." Succubus waved away the thralls.

"Why not one of them?"

"Oh no, my dear. Mere rabble, they are. This one is special."

Into the throne room walked Pharaoh's son Binemwase. Although having escaped adolescence, his features remained boyish. Round, pup-like eyes led to a Grecian-styled nose and a pair of permanently pouting lips. Long tresses of black hair made him look effeminate, but his countenance, although a bit emaciated in the lower body, had enough definition to captivate Neferet.

"Prince Binemwase asked an indulgence of me several days ago."

Neferet's eyes narrowed. "I am listening."

"He wished a sovereign lick, my dear."

"And what exactly is a sovereign lick?"

Succubus bowed to the prince. "She is yours, my lord."

Binemwase stepped forward and removed his flaxen see-through robe, exposing a flaccid cock no longer than Neferet's middle finger. Before she could protest, the prince placed his hands on her shoulders and forced her to kneel, the hobble skirt's leather cutting and binding into her flesh.

"Now, lick our royal member."

To do so, Neferet had to bend at the waist, bringing the needles in the corset's bust into her breasts. She also had to lower her chin a little, thereby driving forward the blades in the hoop, which in turn drew blood from her neck. Although the man's member was dwarfish, his stamina and fortitude proved almost unyielding.

Neferet began by placing the mushroom-shaped helmet upon her lips, pushing against it but not yielding. As the prince grew firm, she parted these most exquisite folds of flesh, sticking out her tongue to tease the cock's tiny hole. Binemwase's ass tightened and he attempted to thrust, but Neferet used her upper teeth to hold him at bay; instead, she used the tip of her tongue to tease the fleshy undercarriage of the cock.

She then opened wider, letting the tongue swirl around the helmet. As she took him inside, the blades and needles continued to spill blood; she fought the temptation to bite down, instead using her cheeks to squeeze the shaft. The sweat and pain were becoming too much, so she impaled herself upon the cock, her chin against his crotch.

When the prince dispensed his imperial seed, Neferet swallowed and then collapsed. Succubus ordered several thralls to take her away.

"I was too much for her," Binemwase said with a smile.

"Indeed," responded Succubus, bowing and taking her leave.

~ ~ ~ ~ ~ ~ ~ ~

After being washed in a shelter known as an ibu, Neferet was taken to an ancient wabet, an embalmer's workshop. It was here that she was coated with oils and herbs and completely wrapped in bandages that contained protective amulets and other charms within several of the folds. Resting upon a stone altar, she waited patiently not for Anubis or the Ferryman, but rather for the scarlet-fleshed demon.

Succubus walked into the room and for a moment contemplated the intricately wrapped woman. She then waved her hands over the mumiyah, removed the golden ceremonial mask, and opened Neferet's mouth so that she once again could walk among the living.

"Are we healing?" asked the she-devil.

"Yes."

"Good." Succubus inspected the mummy. "I hope the wraps are in order."

"They are, as usual." Neferet stared at the ceiling. "That was glorious, she-devil."

"Prince Binemwase was only the beginning."

"Oh?"

Succubus nodded. "In Abydos, there is a frigid priestess in dire need of melting. . . ."

Showing Shana

Every other autumn Crimson Succubus held a pony exhibition in the stronghold of Sanguine, her most exquisite residence. Within Sanguine's vast grounds were a number of stables, and at the apex of these liveries there sat a mammoth circle made of stone.

Dressed from head to toe in equestrian gear made of black latex and red leather, Crimson Succubus cracked her long tail and immediately the human pony galloped around the stone circle, her spiked leather boots clopping to an off-center cadence. The observers took note of the exquisite creature and cheered.

Her faced wrapped in a leather cowl, the pony tussled her auburn mane, her ersatz ears falling back as she did so. Placing her long arms on her luscious hips, she shook her well-groomed tail, its movement garnishing another round of applause and articulated praise.

Without warning, one of the guests interrupted the show. Snapping a crop between muscular hands, Lord Draco stepped into the circle and grabbed the pony's bridle. With one swift tug he pulled it back, the bit tearing into the woman's delicate lips.

"Worry not, little one, Draco means you no harm. I wish only to inspect you from, shall we say, a more intimate perspective."

With his right hand Draco cupped one of the pony's breasts. He gave the honey-filled teat a taut pinch, the leather corset crackling as he did so. Not satisfied, he slapped the human horse's firm bottom, his palm bouncing off the tanned leather.

"Pity, a true mare." He inserted his tongue into her ear, the lingua's tip circling the auricle's intricate crevices with ease. "Still, you are a delectable thing."

"By your leave, Lord." Succubus stepped forward and placed a delicate hand on Draco's inflamed shoulder. "Shana is more than a mere mare. She also is a stallion, a bronco to be savored."

Incredulous, Draco rubbed his crotch against Shana's skin-covered bottom. "No stallion has such round, firm cheeks, my dear Succubus." He pumped his pelvis several times, the bulge lost in the pony's crack. "A feast for any man."

"Reach around," Succubus said with a grin.

Draco did so. "My kind of horse," he said, giving the pony's secret treasure a formidable squeeze.

"She is wild, Lord, and not easily tamed. Care to break her?"

Draco turned and faced the audience. The throng produced red handkerchiefs, waving them in support of the task ahead. The massive man laughed, unbuttoned his trousers, and produced a thick, slightly upturned cock. The crowd went wild.

His cock bouncing side to side, Draco led the pony to a post, where he tied the bridle around the horizontal board. Standing behind Shana, he eased her down so her elbows rested on the wood. He then skinned off her pants enough to expose her luscious ass, but nothing more.

As the crowd roared, Draco licked the palm of his hand and then thrust it between the cheeks. In response, Shana kicked out, her left boot connecting with Draco's thigh. The man let out a roar, his hands clasping the pony's hips.

"Go ahead. Buck, my spirited beauty!"

Pulling her cheeks apart as far as they would go, Draco thrust forward, his cock slamming into her unyielding brown button. Shana neighed, her back arching and her dominant thigh kicking out again. Draco was prepared, however, keeping his legs together as he thrust again, this time piercing her orifice. As he pushed the

81

advantage, the bloated mushroom head disappearing from view, Shana's fragile cock came into view. Soft yet sinewy, it bounced to Draco's thrusting rhythms.

Her kicks no longer connecting, Shana began to buck, her back flexing up and down while her ass moved from side to side. Like a true horseman Draco held on, his hands digging into the pony's hips and his pelvis in line with each buck and plunge. To further demonstrate his prowess, Draco lifted one hand into the air and increased his rhythm, his cock's shaft driving in and out of the pony's quarter-horse bottom.

Spent, Shana leaned heavily on the horizontal post. Draco withdrew, placing his cock lengthwise between the pony's cheeks. There he exploded, alabaster liquid covering the small of her back and dripping onto her leather-clad thighs. Pushing her away, Draco fell on all fours and crawled under Shana. As the pony reached climax, Draco was there to savor the horse's virile cream.

Licking his lips, Lord Draco stood up and faced the rabble. "By all that is unholy, I must have this creature!"

Succubus shook her head. "She is only for show, Lord Draco."

The brawny man grinned. "I beg forgiveness, dearest Succubus."

"Still," she considered. "A pony should be set free, at least every once in a while."

The she-devil walked over to Shana and held out a sugar cube. The pony bent her head down and with her lips took the morsel. Succubus untied the bridle and with great fanfare handed the reins to Draco.

"Thralls, attend me," the she-devil yelled.

At once seven muscular men were at Succubus's side.

"Bring the buggy. Lord Draco is to be escorted to the stables."

Draco beamed, his cock becoming stone again.

Within the pony's leather crotch-bag there also stirred a cock. As the thralls hooked up Shana to the two-wheeled wagon, she licked the iron bit in her mouth, anticipating the defilement she would experience in the stables moments from now.

Pygmalion's Debt

The Greeks often told a story about a lonely king of Cyprus who, because he was disgusted with the faults of ordinary women, labored for many years upon a statue that closely resembled the great goddess Aphrodite. King Pygmalion's masterpiece was so perfect in every way that he fell in love with the sculpture, spurning all female mortals. For years he spent his hours with the figurine, loving it the best he could.

Although the Greeks believed Aphrodite looked down from Mount Olympus and took pity upon the hewer of stone, in truth it was Crimson Succubus who ascended from the burning light and brought life to the ivory sculpture. Pygmalion named the newly born woman Galatea and at once set to marry her. As always with the she-devil, however, there was a price to pay. Pygmalion signed a pact in his own blood, but Succubus failed to claim her favor during the king's long reign.

Death was of no solace to Pygmalion, for the daughter of Lillith at last beckoned him back to the world of the living.

~ ~ ~ ~ ~ ~ ~ ~

Sitting next to the Cocytus River in the Underworld, Pygmalion opened his eyes and found yet another block of marble before him. Standing up, he took hammer and chisel in hand and stepped forward. At once the stone shattered. Aching to create at any cost, Pygmalion dropped to his knees and reached for any piece before him. But Hades was a cruel god; from the sky descended a pair of harpies whose talons ripped at the sculptor's tender flesh. Curled up in a ball, Pygmalion sobbed as the Hounds of Zeus picked up every scrap of rock they could find.

When Pygmalion at last elected to abandon his malaise, he sat up and wiped his forehead. He looked toward the usual site expecting to find another tempting obelisk of marble, but there was no column there. Instead, a crimson-colored female with leathery wings and a spiked tail stood upon the verdant grass, her eyes shimmering like the ripples in the River of Lamentation.

"You, is it?" The artist stood on trembling thighs. "What can you teach Poseidon's brother that he does not already know?"

Crimson Succubus brushed aside some black hair from a curled brow. "You know why I am here. But I am not like Hades, so I tell you this: Do this little thing I ask and I will take you from here. I know of a place."

"You mean I can leave Cocytus?"

"You shall drink from the river Lethe and you will remember no more."

"You promise much, but I do not wish to be like Tityos."

"I shall take the vulture and sting it before it claims you, dear Pygmalion." To accentuate her claim, Succubus rattled her tail.

"Then name this thing, she-devil."

The two walked along the river's edge until they reached its rapids. Pygmalion sat on an ancient tree stump, his hands cupping his heavily bearded face. Succubus stood before him, her arms outspread. Closing her eyes, the she-devil called upon the lightning, with several thunderbolts answering her beckoning. Without a cloud in the sky it began raining, the droplets sizzling cold upon the stone carver's body.

The demon then fell to her knees and plunged both hands into the earth, her fingers wrestling with clods of sand, earth, and clay. As she labored, Pygmalion looked askew, for before his eyes the demon was forming a new life.

As quickly as it had come, the rain went away. Stepping back, Succubus stared at her creation. As tall as Athena, the sculptured woman rivaled the countenance of even Aphrodite. A long mane of raven hair teased slightly red skin. Two sanguine eyes stared at Pygmalion's eyes, and in that instant her slit-like lips parted and a long, wickedly shaped tongue licked up and down. She was slender, almost emaciated, and her body was unusually neutral. She had broad shoulders and sinewy arms, but her breasts were full and round, their nipples bright red and pointed. Her hips were almost nonexistent, but her thighs were muscular and her calves contoured well.

"This is Shana," Succubus said.

The woman bowed, her left thigh moving back as she bent at the waist.

"This is Pygmalion, dear."

"Pygmalion," the girl croaked, her cadence dripping with poison.

"You know what to do, carver."

Pygmalion stood directly in front of Shana, their eyes locked on one another. Without any fanfare, the sculptor knelt and gently parted the woman's thighs. Shana gasped, but before she could say anything, Pygmalion spread her slit apart, forming the fingers on both hands in the shape of a triangle. Sticking his tongue out, he shoved it deep into her crevice, the pink walls vibrating upon contact. Shana dropped her hands onto his shoulders, her fingernails digging deep into his tender flesh.

Despite the pain, Pygmalion was not swayed. Instead, he drove his tongue even deeper, opening his mouth as wide as he could. Once inside, he began flicking the tip up and down then from side to side. He found her bell and incessantly rang it, almost bringing Shana to tears in the process. His lips locked around the love chasm, he probed as far as he could into the abyss, drinking from its pond of sweet nectar.

Shana tightened, climax building within her gut and churning out slowly through her extremities like a whirlpool under Poseidon's wrath. To help it along, Pygmalion eased his middle finger into her remaining orifice. Stifling a scream, Shana flexed her cheek muscles, which in turn brought down her crotch upon the carver's face. Pygmalion pushed up, straddling her so that her toes barely touched the ground.

The release was impossible, for as she achieved orgasm a thick, honey-textured liquid oozed from within, at first choking the hewer of stone. Wiping his mouth free, Pygmalion wanted very much to run, but he remained stalwart.

"Now, Pygmalion," ordered Crimson Succubus.

Cupping both hands, Pygmalion caught the fluid in his palms. As the liquid settled on his skin, it took on the aspect of flesh tinged with a hint of umber. As the elixir continued to flow, Pygmalion began to mold and fashion it with his bare fingers. At first the icon appeared lifeless, but as he worked feverishly it began taking on a life of its own.

Dexterous digits formed an oblong shaft, thick and round, at the end of which was fashioned a mushroom-shaped head. Using his pinky, he made a hole at the chanterelle's apex; from it more nectar dripped, but this time the fluid was thick and alabaster. Below the dagger-length shaft Pygmalion crafted a bulbous sac that was soft to the touch.

Spent, Pygmalion fell to one side.

Shana looked down and admired her newfound manhood. Her face and breasts remained, but now her bell was a morel and her lifeblood hung below. Delicate hands squeezed the shaft and instantly the rod responded, the shaft engorged and the head turning a most appealing shade of purple.

Succubus knelt before the primordial phallus, her mouth watering.

~ ~ ~ ~ ~ ~ ~ ~

At the aft of a small boat stood a cloaked steersman at the rudder, the orbs within its hood changing colors like a rainbow in the sky. Pygmalion sat at the forward, his eyes searching the riverbank. As for Succubus, she sat in the middle, her leathery wings folded into her body.

"I believe it is here, she-devil."

"What is here?" she teased.

"Lethe."

"I know the river, but you are not destined for it."

Pygmalion turned around, his face a scowl. "But I kept my word."

Succubus cackled. "Yes, you did." With a longer fingernail she pointed to an island beyond the horizon.

Upon the beach stood a frail women dressed in an ivory robe. As the boat drew closer, she stood on her toes and began waving a bleached ascot. Pygmalion caught a glimpse of her, his eyes a chasm of delight.

"But she was not mortal."

"Although pitch black and rotten at its impious core, a heart does beat within the thorax of the solemn Hades." Succubus rubbed the artist's back. "A gentle reminder about the maiden Persephone and abdication on his part soon followed."

Pygmalion's face grew soft again. "Why do this? After all, you are much more vehement than the gorgons and the furies. I have witnessed your deeds—all come with a price."

"So they do." Succubus hugged herself. "I will have need of you again, someday."

The sculptor chuckled. "I see." He turned to stare at his love, who now had grown closer. "What of Shana?"

"Oh, I have plans for her."

"Upon the land of Zeus and the water of Poseidon?"

"Yes. Hera cannot wait for the time when her husband comes to seduce the exquisite Shana. And so will mortal man fall for such beings, those who are neither man nor woman but offer the best of both ambrosia and nectar."

"I understand now why Hades helped you."

Succubus licked the back of Pygmalion's neck. "You are no fool, dearest."

The Demon Chronicles: Leshi

Crimson Succubus motioned the eonist Shana to strip naked, which the thrall did as quickly as she could.

"You have failed me yet again, harlot," Succubus began, her eyes sanguine and her wings spread wide. "You must be punished for this transgression."

Succubus walked over to a large mahogany chest, lifted the lid, and produced a beautiful black dress. From the neckline to the upper thighs the silk dress had pleats that ran a dagger's length deep. The sleeveless garment had a tanned leather belt, the inside of which was lined with tiny hairs, each delicately sewed into the hide.

"Put this on."

Shana eased into the dress, letting it fall onto her curvy frame. It was tight about her breasts, and as she attempted to adjust it, the pleats brushed against her nipples, inflaming them so much they ached. Taking a deep breath, she shifted her weight from her left hip to the right; in so doing, more of the dress's pleats tickled her cock and balls. Her scrotum tightened, growing slightly cold, while her cock expanded, with each tingle of the plaits making it stiffer and stiffer.

Wanting very badly to remove the dress, Shana made to lift it over her head, only to be stopped by Succubus. With a devious smile the she-devil brought Shana's arms back down and then cinched the belt around her middle. As soon as Succubus buckled the chastity lock Shana began giggling, for the hair within the belt sent infinite reverberations through her spine.

"Mirth, from you?" Succubus stared at the slave. "Perhaps some bastinado is in order?"

With little effort Succubus pushed Shana onto a wooden rack. After binding the thrall's hands and feet with metal restraints, Succubus walked once again to the mahogany chest and brought out a metal box, within which was a most elaborate white feather.

"Mistress, no!"

"No?" It was Succubus's turn to laugh. "My little maid has forgotten herself. Tsk-tsk. Perhaps a more dire experience is in order."

Shana began struggling, the folds on the dress following each move like a tormentor's dexterous hands. Tears rolled down her face, staining the wood, as Succubus put away the feather and placed a red mushroom between her thighs.

"Shana, I want you to meet Leshi. He's a very nice demon, as you will soon see."

From out of the mushroom came a tiny creature with glimmering red skin, a singular horn and eye, a mouthful of pointed teeth, and a slender, almost emaciated body. The demon stared at Shana.

"My, big bosom and long dirk," Leshi said, staring up at Shana's considerable member. "Leshi likes."

Using little suction cups on his fingers and toes, Leshi began climbing up Shana's balls and then her cock, his ascent driving her crazy with titillating sensations. Leshi's tickling forced Shana to move, thereby activating the dress, which in turn drove her to the point of insanity.

Standing on Shana's purple helmet, Leshi stuck out his tongue. "This is nothing, lascivious human. Leshi show you something now."

Headfirst, Leshi dove into Shana's cock hole. She tensed as the diminutive abomination crawled inside her cock. The suction cups on the demon's fingers and toes once again stimulated her, only this time the sensations came from within. Shana stifled a shriek; she could feel an ejaculation building, yet the creature had a way of preventing the alabaster fluid from exploding out her throbbing hole.

Insane laughter filled the chamber as Leshi continued exploring from within Shana's most interesting countenance, in particular her well-polished and taut button.

~ ~ ~ ~ ~ ~ ~ ~

At dawn, Crimson Succubus stepped into Shana's room. Before the she-devil closed the door, the slave was out of bed and on her knees, with eyes downcast and chin tilted down.

"Would you like to hear something funny?" Succubus grinned.

"Yes, Mistress."

"Very good, demimonde. Now, stand up. We have much to do."

Succubus handed Shana a white dress.

"Mistress?"

Succubus reached for the door. "Today's demon is Umin."

Shana looked at the inside of the garment. Uncounted numbers of tiny needles lined the gown.

The she-devil whirled around. "His virtue is pain."

As they walked down a dark corridor, Shana could not help but wonder if Succubus would ever run out of demons.

"Remember Christ?" Succubus muttered after scanning the servant's feeble intellect. "And his encounter with Legion?"

Soft laughter filled the ebon atmosphere of the corridor as two shadows disappeared into the viscous ether.

Revelation

Surrounded by mountains of parchment and tattered tomes, Thomas Aquinas stared into the darkness, his eyes mesmerized by the vortex of contemplation. But this self-induced hypnotism did not last long, for it was soon shattered by an undulating body just outside the haze of his thoughts.

Crimson Succubus, adorned with a variety of bells, danced about in the dark. The she-devil's well-rounded hips grinded from side to side as breasts heaved and hands and legs wove captivating spells. Aquinas was far from moved.

"Be gone, demon," he bellowed. "You are sexless."

Suddenly, the sanguine demon was at his side, her long tail caressing his dormant member. "But you are not."

"Masturbation is a mortal sin."

"Oh, I agree, dearest theologian." Succubus tightened her whipcord tail about his cock, its barbed end teasing the member's sensitive underside. "But unlike that harlot in San Giovanni, I will never be driven away by your sorcerer's tongue and steady resolve."

Aquinas moaned. "What are you?"

Succubus blasted hot air into the philosopher's ear. "The reason for penance."

~ ~ ~ ~ ~ ~ ~ ~

The following morning, Aquinas abandoned the writing of his great work, the *Summa Theologica*.

"I cannot go on," he said later. "All that I have written seems to me like so much straw compared to what I have seen and what has been revealed to me."

She Comes in Dreams

There is no piousness in dreams. . . .

Round and round the rosary goes
Tightening and tightening
Row after row

Whispers and whispers, the prayers are spent—
The priest, he cries out
His abhorred lament

Stiffer and stiffer his member becomes
Leathery wings at the window
The seduction's begun

Twisting and twisting, the passion's undone
She-devil and clergyman
Wrestle as one

Screaming and screaming, his seed is released
Stains on the rosary
Stigmata's the beast

Sanctity is but passion bound. . . .

- Mytoessa's Tales -

The Essence of Magic

Mytoessa opened her crystal-green eyes and immediately felt the sting of raindrops. The tree she huddled under offered some protection from the storm, but a sweet-smelling secretion from its spade-shaped leaves, when combined with rainfall, created a biting emulsion that the wild folk within Nimwood used on their arrows and spears. The emulsion was not lethal, but it was most uncomfortable, particularly when it came into contact with tender or deeply pierced flesh.

The cloudburst intensified, with several thunderclaps bringing the young woman out of her light slumber. Yawning, she stood up and moved into a narrow clearing, where she allowed the rain to wash away the stinging concoction from her naked body. The raindrops proved a bit too chilly, however, so she wrapped a drenched cloak about her thin frame. Mytoessa began walking through the thick forest, her eyes wide as she inhaled the intoxicating smells of the damp forest.

For as long as could be remembered Nimwood had stood along the eastern slopes of the Enlilic Mountains. Although the fairies and other wild folk within the forest accepted Mytoessa as one of their own, the woman with tresses of bright red hair actually belonged to the world of men. Born in the caves that face the southern fjords along the coast of Icetock, Mytoessa was neither named nor sired amongst her people. Barbaric invaders from the forsaken land known as Muspell had massacred most of the cave dwellers shortly after her birth. The few who had survived the onslaught, mostly women and children, were sold into slavery, but the wee thing now known as Mytoessa was overlooked and left behind to starve.

Close to Nimwood's apex, the green-eyed girl quickened her pace, her callus-soled feet furtive enough to leave fallen leaves and fledgling foliage undisturbed. As she stepped into a clearing, several trees groaned. Mytoessa's eyebrows went up. She unsheathed a long dual-edged blade hanging on her back. Squinted eyes scanned the trees and their kin. Nothing dared move.

"I know you are there," she whispered. "You have disturbed the slumber of the Old Ones."

Mytoessa grinned. Although she was a daughter of men, her blood had mixed with the wild folk of the forest, and as a result she freely associated with everything, from the trees, rocks, and flowers to things stranger still. Long and painful had been the lessons she had endured in Nimwood, but now, at the age of ascension, Mytoessa understood well their worth, particularly when it came to her continued survival.

That she had survived at all in such an unforgiving environment was a miracle. As an infant, Mytoessa lived inside a cave for an untold time, with only her spirit and will to sustain her meager existence. One morning the dryad Nimue, after which the forest had been named, heard the child's desperate cries while she walked along the edge of the darkest of woods. The dryad entered the cave to investigate. She found the baby, and after feeding and caring for its many welts and bruises, brought it before the wild folk who, although apprehensive, agreed to help rear the child in the ways of nature.

Under Nimue's tutelage, Mytoessa had learned the ways of the earth and its variety of occupants. Such intense saturation changed her spirit and body, and in some ways she had become like one of the wild folk. Although mortal, she showed not her age, nor did afflictions or diseases affect her constitution. Her healing powers were significant, so much so that few weapons could cause permanent injury. And her senses were vibrant and acute—not even the stealthiest of predators could come upon her unaware. So it was with her stalker now.

"Show yourself before the Old Ones wrap their tendrils about your flesh and squeeze your blood so that it mingles with the ravenous soil," she said, her blade lowered. "The night betrays you, for you are transparent to these eyes."

From between a pair of thick and gnarled trees emerged a most hideous sight. The monstrosity stood almost tree height, but it was hunched over, its bald head buried into its shoulders and its chin curiously resting on its chest. The thing's face consisted of two massive bull horns, a pair of narrow eyes filled with swirls of sanguine fluid, a flared nose, and a maw filled with dagger-sized teeth. As for its frame, it was bloated and cumbersome, its fat hands dragging along the brush while trunk-thick legs thundered the earth. Black skin shimmered in the rain, even though most of the precipitation seemed to shy away from the behemoth.

"What does a fae need with steel?" the thing asked, a heavily coiled fingernail pointing at the young woman's blade.

"I am no fae. And what need do you have for stealth?"

"Not fae?" The creature chuckled. "The trees of Nimwood are fickle. No matter. I come with a message for Nimue's heir. Do you know of her?"

"An unclothed behemoth who travels under the light of the moon?" She took a step back. "I am the one you seek: my name is Mytoessa, and I am one with Nimue. Deliver your message."

"I am called Vespar, thrall to Skallagrim, the bony one. My necronomatic lord wishes to march his warriors through Nimwood, but he knows well that this is the enchanting Nimue's realm and that she abhors steel and its kin. He also realizes that the wild folk may hinder the army's progress. I come without weapons or armor to honor your mistress's will."

"Indeed," Mytoessa nodded, her eyes staring at the massive member dangling between Vespar's thighs, its toadstool-shaped head as thick as one of the thing's kneecaps. "But if this is so, your master also knows that nothing will move Nimue from her rectitude, not even the darkness that imbues the bony one. So

100

inform your master that he must find another way. Nimwood does not condone violence of any kind."

The girl's words were far from welcome. Vespar lifted its arms up, straightening its back, and stiffening its legs to hold up its barrel-shaped trunk. With a thunderous roar the behemoth brought down both fists like a hammer to an anvil, the resultant reverberations upon the earth uprooting several of the smaller trees and throwing into chaos the wildlife in the surrounding area. Cicadas buzzed about, frogs belched, wolves howled, and even some fairies scintillated along the edge of the clearing, their color changes snapping and crackling as they floated upon dense air.

"Shall I raze this forest, little one?" Vespar bellowed. "Lay down that blade. That steel, it shall betray you."

Mytoessa thrust the sword's tip into Vespar's chest. Although the blade struck flesh, it did not penetrate. It was as if the steel had struck stone. Bewildered, the girl thrust again and again, each time the blade easily deflected. Vespar chuckled, its mammoth arms akimbo.

"My kind lives in harmony with steel. It is said our hide was forged within the same kiln, tempered much like the elfin blades of old. Has not the lovely Nimue taught you the ways of trolls, little one?"

Before Mytoessa could formulate an answer, the troll used the thumb and forefinger of its left hand to clasp the sword's tip. Vespar wrenched the sword from the girl's hands. The creature then picked up and held the weapon by the hilt. With care it placed the sword's edge along the subdued head of its dangling cock. Along the thick hide the troll ran the sword's length, sparks of steel lighting up the darkness.

"Your blade needs little attention—the edge is pristine." Without care it tossed aside the sword and moved closer. "And my flesh is but a sharpening stone for such as that. Have you nothing to say to me now?" Vespar's eyes widened as the girl's breathing became erratic. "Tell me where I might parlay with Nimue, little one, for her heir lacks the tongue of diplomacy."

"Never."

"I need not use violence to obtain what I need." The troll leered, its left hand clasping around the redheaded girl while the right ripped away her cloak. "Squeezing this exquisite body of yours shall be sufficient."

Only on several occasions had Nimue mentioned trolls, which the wild folk considered baneful and loathsome. There were many types of trolls, most of them inhabiting the wastelands in Muspell or roaming through the marshes in desolate Stord. Amongst the most dangerous of trolls was the stone troll, which gave loyalty to no one but rather sold its allegiance for wealth and power. It was said its hide, though soft to the touch, could not be harmed by blunt or piercing weapons, nor could most magic influence or stay such a beast's rampage. But natural magic, that was something entirely different.

"Squeeze me, will you?" Mytoessa relaxed her body. "Do your worst, but first grant this little one a request. It is a harmless supplication, of course."

Mytoessa rubbed her fingertips against her forehead and then moved them down her cheeks, neck, and breasts. Her hands traveled further, until her nails pulled apart her thighs and rested within the heated orifice. Dexterous fingers then ran along the slit's length, moistening her engorged cleft. The troll sniffed the air, its nose flared.

"I am no fool, elfling. You have the taint of the dryad upon those tender lips. It is said such a taint can bring upon some a madness from which there is no recovery."

"Does this blight of confusion apply to trolls as well? I would have believed differently."

102

"You are shrewd. Still, there is some truth to your words."

Releasing her, Vespar squared its shoulders and placed its massive fists a little below its bloated ribcage. Softened eyes assessed the little thing. Although the troll's face revealed little, its member spoke volumes, for it went from wrinkled and flaccid to smooth and stiff. Nonchalantly one of the troll's hands grasped the stiffened rod, rounded fingertips running the length of the shaft as melon-sized testicles like a pendulum swung back and forth to a consistent rhythm.

Mytoessa watched as the troll pleasured itself. Aroused, the young woman also feared for her life, for the monstrosity's cock was eight times larger than even the greatest of men. Merely accommodating the rod's helmet would rip her to pieces. Perhaps it had been a mistake to release her scent, but there was no known means to nullify such a sensual discharge. She looked to the sky but could find no alternative course of action. Staring at the troll's cock anew, however, gave her an idea.

"Listen to my request." Mytoessa knelt before the troll's loins, the fingernails from both of her hands digging into the cock's dark brown helmet. "You cannot take me, for such subjugation would surely mean a quick death. But allow me to take you. I hunger for the nectar within you, for the essence of life brings to me a wellspring of joy and desire. Let me draw it forth, I beseech you."

"If I do as you ask," the troll said in a trembling voice, "will you tell me where I may find your mistress?"

"Yes," Mytoessa cooed. "I give you my word."

The troll grasped the base of its member with both hands. "You may find siphoning my essence a challenge, sprite. We trolls relinquish our nectar so rarely."

"I sincerely hope it is as you claim," she countered, smacking her lips.

"No more talk, little one. Demonstrate your prowess."

With a tug Mytoessa brought the huge cock to her face. She opened her mouth as wide as possible and used her lips to moisten the periphery of the helmet's opening. She then focused on the opening itself, using her tongue to flick along the edges of the sensitive orifice. Not satisfied, she lifted the cock above her head, her tongue licking the length of the split and nibbling at its curious tinderbox. Vespar's burgeoning moans turned to low-pitched bellows sodden with supplication.

As the troll swallowed in an attempt to regain some of its composure, Mytoessa pushed the rod down, her fingernails digging into the shaft. She climbed onto the cock, her breasts, gut, and clit rubbing the head and shaft as her fingers tore at its base. The troll could take no more: it arched its back and prepared to release. The young woman noticed the creature's stiffening stance and in response slipped off and released its cock, letting it bob in front of her face.

"Continue, strumpet!" the troll exclaimed. "This cannot be the end."

"No, it is not."

Mytoessa crawled between the troll's bowlegged thighs, where she sat up and placed her face behind its low-hanging sac. Digging her nails into the tender flesh there, she licked from the base of its puckered button down to the border of the low-hanging sac. Once again Vespar groaned with delight, the resonance within its bones vibrating the testicles within the membranous pouch. Mytoessa traveled upward, and upon her reverse trip she no longer licked but rather used her teeth to nip at the sensitive flesh.

Lying down, she clasped one of the troll's orbs and brought it to her lips. Like an infant entertaining itself with the round end of a rattle, the young woman bounced the globe on her lips, at length wrapping her arms around it and biting into the toughest of the meat.

Vespar dug its conical fingers into its cheeks and mouth in an attempt to stifle a scream. For a second time the troll felt its body suffuse with warmth. The anticipation made it stiffen like one of the many trees that surrounded the couple. As climax blossomed, however, Mytoessa released the monstrosity once more, disrupting its ability to erupt.

"I shall kill you!" it howled.

Mytoessa was undeterred by Vespar's outburst. Indeed, its anger seemed to create additional lust within the woman, for she crawled from underneath its sac, stood up, and fell upon its still-rigid member, her breasts rubbing against the shaft while her slit teased the head's opening. Like oil Vespar's wrath trickled down its brow, chest, and thighs. The troll's blood boiled anew.

"Patience, Vespar," she whispered. "This is a game, after all. The rapids of your nectar increase in intensity with each assault, thus weakening the integrity of the dam that is your strength of will. Such will be the next rush that the dam no longer will abate the water's strength. Think of the resultant burst as the dam falls at last."

The troll snickered. "You are clever, little dryad. It is true—the ache inside me is so great that little can contain it." The troll used its hands to bounce the cock up and down while Mytoessa held on. "The dam shall crumble and my nectar shall run free at last!"

Mytoessa ran her fingernails along the cock's shaft while bouncing her slit off the mushroom-shaped head. Vespar's heat returned, but this time the sprite did not cease her attentions, but rather intensified them. Arching its back, Vespar released its cock and threw its hands to the sky as it felt the dam within collapse and the river of nectar from its aching globes at last found the might to break through.

"Yes," it hissed through clenched teeth. "By Skallagrim's aura of darkness, yes!"

But the eruption was not to be, the troll learned as its eyes were set aflame from what it saw in the sky.

"No!" it shrieked.

Up in the sky, the clouds parted as dawn came to Nimwood. The sun's first rays touched the trees, Mytoessa, and the troll. The trees and the young woman rejoiced at the orb's life-granting heat and light. But for the troll, daylight was bane. Vespar turned to stone before its rigid cock could relinquish one drop of its precious nectar.

Curled in the grassy clearing, Mytoessa wiped her mouth and wept.

~ ~ ~ ~ ~ ~ ~ ~

Two women sat on the soft but strong roots of a massive and ancient tree known as Gudin. The dryad Nimue was tall and wasp-like, her shimmering silver hair accented a face with a pair of wondrous eyes, a half-moon shaped nose, and mouthwatering lips. Next to her sat Mytoessa, a sword resting on her knees.

"What troubles you, my darling?" the nymph asked, extraordinarily long fingers playing with Mytoessa's locks.

"Mother, the taste of violence lingers about me, its miasma in the very air that I breathe. That thing over there—that troll—it brought violence to our home. At first I used the blade, but when it failed me, I resorted to my charms and the very sun to subdue my adversary. I am ashamed."

"I sense great pain in your father's blade, for in his hands it brought down many lives. And I sense this same pain within you, sweet child, but do not succumb to shame. Violence is to be abhorred, but wild folk must often defend their home. Many

106

select distraction, enchantment, and slumber as weapons, for these leave no lasting damage."

"So magic becomes a weapon?"

"Nature is a weapon, dearest, from the seedpod that bursts its sapling through the earth to the wolf that fells its prey with tooth and claw. Nothing remains pristine, not even fairy."

"Not even you, Mother?"

"Not even me, darling."

The young woman frowned. "My view of the world, it has changed."

"Its countenance makes you fair." Nimue giggled, her mirth resonating like blossoming flower petals against her daughter's skin. "As for the troll, it slumbers in peace, and perhaps such torment will one day enable it to stir to life. But its life will be one of misery, so perhaps it is for the best that stillness has claimed it for the moment. I know so little of such matters, my darling."

"Vespar is not dead?"

"No, dearest. The creature abides, of that be certain."

Mytoessa stared at the creature frozen still in the clearing. At the base of its stone cock was a small nest made of twigs, feathers, and dry grass. Several chicks sat in the nest, their insistent beaks blindly searching the air as in unison they chirped for their mother. The hatchlings did not wait long, for moments later a small bright red bird landed on the statue's bloated cock-head, a worm in her mouth.

Closing her eyes, Mytoessa felt the frozen troll shudder.

"It abides, Mother." She clasped her sword tightly. "It abides."

A Gift of Revenge

Even the oldest creatures of Nimwood could not easily remember how long the thick and verdant forest had served as a haven for all manner of creature. But a few did recollect that the woodland had not always been as friendly, for there had been a time in which ancient abominations traversed Nimwood's delicate soil, leaving a memory of evil in their wake. Slowly, foliage healed the land but still other living things avoided the place, until one summer morning a young dryad by the name of Nimue dared to tread the blighted soil. With outstretched hands she cleansed the air and healed the earth, making it possible for the wild folk to return from their long exile to the forest they once called home.

At first Nimue called everywhere home, but soon she found a special place in the forest to call her own. At the center of these lush woodlands stood a massive tree, its intertwined branches shaped by the wheels of time into the semblance of an overarching umbrella. Nimue spent most of her time here, and when the tree had grown accustomed to her ways she claimed the place as her own. In time, Nimue became queen of the wild folk. And so things were, until the time of snow, when smoke filled the sky and death scented the wind.

The horde came upon Nimwood at dusk. Wild folk living at the peripheries of the forest sent word about thick wafts of smoke along the western slopes of the Enlilic Mountains, smoke that grew thicker as the sun gave way to the moon. By the time the disturbing news reached the ears of Nimue the hideous abominations known as the Boggarts had come down from the mountains, their numbers not so easily counted.

As the principal protector of Nimwood, Nimue left the sanctuary of her tree and stood in a clearing filled with tall grass and volcanic rock. At her side was a young woman with thick tresses of dark brown hair and crystal-green eyes. The wild folk had named her Mytoessa.

Although the daughter of a human male, her blood had mixed freely with that of the wild folk, and as a result she was kin to the fairies of the forest. She empathized with everything, from the obsidian rocks and prismatic flowers to sentinel trees and things stranger still. Mytoessa knew little of her early days. Her life had begun when Nimue brought her into the forest to rear as one of her own. Although the wild folk rejected the infant at first, at length they agreed to help Nimue raise the child in the ways of nature.

Unlike her charge, Nimue possessed a vague countenance, which much like vapor was felt more than seen. The fairy stood unusually tall, statuesque even amongst the elves, and was slender from head to foot. She wore no clothes, her ethereal skin scintillating like evening dew. Silver eyes shimmered like crystal facets caressed by light. Golden tresses of hair crackled to a gentle breeze.

The hearts of both women grew heavy as the horde of Boggarts ripped its way through the edge of the forest. Called goblins by the people of the west, the Boggarts had been tainted by the Bony One, a wraith whose ancient name was Skallagrim. Once elfin sorcerers and warriors, the Boggarts had been seduced by avarice, lechery, and vehemence. Like their phantom master the elves grew corrupt, so much so that their once wondrous aspect took on horrid qualities.

Locks of platinum or golden hair gave way to clumps of thin, brassy coils, enchanted eyes turned sharp and shallow, and tender mouths transformed into leers filled with dagger-shaped teeth. They abandoned magical armor and took up skins, with most of the creatures preferring little if any clothing. Hardening their bodies through hideous rituals of pain, the Boggarts selected heavy slashing or smashing weaponry. They disdained the bow and the other elegant weapons favored by their distant brothers.

The leader of the repulsive horde stepped forward, his eyes narrow, spittle lining a flaccid lower lip. Nimue gazed back. He had a massive face with narrow, darkened eyes, a fat nose, and a slit mouth. A hairless, grayish head sported the remains of a helmet. Numerous ingots decorated a pair of thick, pointed ears. He was unusually tall and lean, his muscles blending into one another, and wore only the remnants of a tunic and a pair of leather boots with iron spurs.

"Step aside, tree-woman," the leader said in a high-pitched rasp. "We march toward Muspell on my master's errand."

"You may pass, but disturb this place no more."

"What say you to me?" The Boggart clutched a curved blade in both hands. "We are Skallagrim's thralls—we do his will. You hold no sway here."

"Skallagrim does not concern me. However, your iron and steel disturb this place. Sheath your weapons and tread lightly if you are to pass. Otherwise, take to the mountains, where you may ruin without measure."

Before Nimue could say or do anything more, the Boggart swung the blade. The sharp edge cut clean through the dryad's neck. Mytoessa screamed as she watched her mother's frail body fall to the ground as her head landed in a patch of damp leaves and vibrant flowers.

"My master's blackened edge!" the leader bellowed as he held the sword toward a darkening sky. "Not even the wild folk's queen can stay its course!"

From out of the forest emerged all manner of wild folk. They gathered around the fallen dryad, tears scintillating under a twilight sun. Mytoessa knelt before Nimue and wept.

As the Boggart army resumed its march through Nimwood, the leader walked over to Mytoessa. Hovering above her, he pushed back a tanned pelt to reveal his heavily chiseled loins. He turned his head to one side as he studied the woman's flushed countenance.

"Tears are wasted here, little one" he growled. "You would do well to seek revenge for your queen instead."

"Revenge?" Mytoessa looked up, here eyes gleaming.

"You do not have it in your heart?" The commander stared into her face and grinned. "How can this be?"

"I have only sadness." Mytoessa turned away.

The Boggart crouched. "But you are not fairy."

"It is of no consequence."

"Innocence in your kind is fleeting." The Boggart reached out to touch the girl's face, but she refused to meet his gaze. "I must undo what these creatures of the forest have done. If you were to leave this place your own kind would feed on such innocence, leaving little more than a husk."

The Boggart leader stood up and with gnarled hands clasped Mytoessa's wrists. He lifted her without a struggle and held her close to his chest. The young woman felt the intense heat from his body as blasts of air struck her face. She took in his musky scent as strange feelings coursed through the inside of her skin.

Digging his claws into her hips, he turned her away from him. Mytoessa at first resisted, but the Boggart's strength was too great. Sweat lined her body as the creature eased her downward a little, her golden-skinned bottom exposed to him. Mytoessa gasped as he eased her onto him.

His cock was long and thick, its mushroom-shaped head as large as her own fist. She felt its tip against the lips of her rosebud. The Boggart moved his hips up and down, the motion teasing her lips until they burned like scorched earth. He then eased his cock into her, piercing her walls and breaking through the veil of her innocence. Mytoessa stifled a scream as her slit swallowed the length of his shaft.

Once inside, the Boggart remained still, his flared nostrils taking in the fresh scent of woman. Mytoessa arched her back and pulled her hips forward, his cock slowly emerging from her aroused crevice. She pulled to the point of complete withdrawal, only to impale herself on him again and again.

And then it was the Boggart who took command. Stiffening his legs, he thrust into her time after time, his massive cock working like a battering ram against her tender flesh. Mytoessa rolled her eyes and groaned as the Boggart's pelvis tightened. He wrapped his claws about her breasts and placed his mouth on her shoulder. As Mytoessa reveled in her climax, the Boggart opened his mouth wide and bit into her clavicle.

Spasms of pain shot through Mytoessa's body. Instead of crying out, however, she whirled around, pushed off the creature, and withdrew his sword from its scabbard.

"Revenge," he muttered, his eyes wide. "Take it!"

Mytoessa struck, the blade's tip piercing the Boggart's chest and plunging into his beating heart. As life left him, his cock at last spewed its seed. The miasmic juice spattered onto the ground.

For the longest time Mytoessa knelt before the dead Boggart commander. While she pondered her metamorphosis, the wild folk took Nimue to her tree, where it was believed she would in time heal from the Boggart's wound and once again walk as queen amongst the dwellers of the forest. The fairies and pixies dared not approach Mytoessa, for she had been soiled.

The following morning, Mytoessa walked in the forest, a sword in its scabbard resting on her left hip. Never again would

Nimwood fall victim to another raid. Amongst the sheep there now prowled a wolf.

Mytoessa crouched before a bed of scarlet woodland. She picked one and rubbed the petals along her skin. Deep down, she wished for another horde to come through Nimwood.

"Revenge," she whispered, her hands moving between her damp thighs.

Publication History

- "To the Devil, a Daughter," original to this collection.

- "After Sodom and Gomorra," originally published in *BDSM Café*, B and belle, Editors (April 2005).

- "In Mockery of the Angel of Death," originally published in *Logical Lust*, *XtreXmeX* feature, Captivatex, Editor (March 2005).

- "The Estuary, "originally published in *Logical Lust*, *XtreXmeX* feature, Captivatex, Editor (May 2005).

- "Bringer of Light," original to this collection.

- "Fall of the Grigori," original to this collection.

- "Thelema's Babalon Working: The Contents of a Man's Chalice," original to this collection.

- "War of Words," originally published in *Quickie Feature Gallery*, Erotica Readers and Writers Association, Gary Russell, Editor (July 2005).

- "The Imp of the Perverse," original to this collection.

- "A Monk's Holy Water," original to this collection.

- "The Serpent that cannot be Charmed," original to this collection.

- "Feeding the She-Devil," original to this collection.

- "Of the Wanderer Matronit and Masturbation," original to this collection.

- "Seal of Solomon," originally published in *TreSart's World of Erotica*, TreSart Sioux, Editor (June 2005).

- "Protection from the Night-Strangler," original to this collection.

- "Blaspheming the Tetragrammaton," original to this collection.

- "Amorous'Humor," original to this collection.

- "Loving the Worm," originally published in *Mind Caviar*, Jamie Joy Gatto, Editor (September 2002).

- "Sanguine Maiden," originally published in *Lair of the Shebitch*, LiaCarla, Editor (August 2002). Reprinted in **Erotic Fantasy: Tales of the Paranormal**, Justus Roux, Editor (April 2004).

- "The Demon Chronicles: Kuru-pira," originally published in *Shadow of the Marquis*, Alex Severin, Editor (September 2002).

- "Master of Ropes," originally published in *kristydoll's BDSM Ezine*, Kristydoll, Editor (April 2003).

- "The Demon Chronicles: The Beauty that is Naamah," original to this collection.

- "Branding Nina," originally published in *Blood Moon Zine*, Oceana, Editor (August 2002).

- "Shackled in Perpetuity," originally published in *BDSM Library*, Jinn, Editor (January 2003).

- "Seven Gold Coins for Shana," originally published in *Sauce*Box: The E-zine of Literary Erotica*, Guillermo Bosch, Editor (March 2003). Reprinted by invitation in *Libida*, Dr. Kathleen Van Kirk, VP of Content (July 2004).

- "The Art of Forniphilia," originally published in *Abby's Realm*, Tammy Brennan, Editor (2002).

- "A Night with a Vampire," originally published in *Lair of the Shebitch*, LiaCarla, Editor (October 2002).

- "Eternal Mummy," originally published in *Gromet's Plaza*, Gromet, Editor (June 2002).

- "Showing Shana," originally published in *Nifty Erotic Stories Archive* (August 2002).

- "Pygmalion's Debt," originally published in *Sauce*Box: The E-zine of Literary Erotica*, Guillermo Bosch, Editor (November 2003).

- "The Demon Chronicles: Leshi," originally published in *Nifty Erotic Stories Archive* (June 2002).

- "Revelation," original to this collection.

- "She Comes in Dreams," originally published in *The Emerald Collection*, Rachel, Editor (November 2002).

- "The Essence of Magic," originally published in *Ruthie's Club*, Neil Anthony, Editor (October 2004).

- "A Gift of Revenge," originally published in *Ruthie's Club* for the Sword & Sorcery special edition, Neil Anthony, Editor (April 2005).